'But Gus isn't a long name,' she said.

Aunt Rachel came to her rescue. 'Gus is really Augustus,' she told her. Kate could see why he preferred Gus. 'And Ned is Benedict. Then when Charley was born, Nicky and I thought we'd pick a name beginning with C . . .'

'And then Darius, and then Edward.' The penny dropped, and Kate thought what very peculiar names her cousins had. Alphabet names. Alphabet cousins. 'I suppose my name should be Felicity, really,' she said, biting into a ham roll. 'Or Fiona. You know, to carry on the alphabet.'

ALPHABET COUSINS

Catherine Robinson

RED FOX

A Red Fox Book
Published by Random Century Children's Books
20 Vauxhall Bridge Road, London SW1V 2SA

A division of the Random Century Group

London Melbourne Sydney Auckland
Johannesburg and agencies throughout the world

First published by The Bodley Head Children's Books 1991

Red Fox edition 1992

Copyright © Catherine Robinson 1991

Printed and bound in Great Britain by
Cox & Wyman Ltd, Reading, Berkshire

ISBN 0 09 985400 7

Contents

1

Appleford House

Only one person got off the train this time. A young man, muffled against the chill Devon wind in a long khaki-coloured greatcoat and a multi-coloured scarf, wrapped several times around his neck and ears.

'Barton St Mary!' the guard shouted, self-importantly, and blew his whistle. The train huffed away with a great noise of diesel, as if it really didn't want to stay there any longer. Kate watched as the young man heaved his bag on to his shoulder and strode purposefully towards the bench where she and Mrs Shaddock were sitting, down the platform to the exit. He smiled as he passed them, crinkling his eyes in a friendly way.

'Evenin',' he remarked. 'Cold out.' He had an accent Kate had only ever heard in films; 'local yokel' the girls at school would have called it.

Mrs Shaddock smiled at him, but Kate hunched her shoulders inside her coat and ignored him. He looked quite nice, but you never knew with strangers. Moodily, she started to kick her suitcase, which stood before her on the platform. It was so quiet she could hear the second-hand on the station clock tick round with irritating monotony, and she timed her kicks to come just after the seconds: tick (*kick*), tick (*kick*), tick (*kick*).

'Don't do that, Kathleen love,' Mrs Shaddock told her, but in a kindly voice. 'You'll scuff your shoes, and once that patent leather is scuffed it's ruined.'

Kate scowled, but she stopped kicking. She burrowed her cold hands deeper into her pockets, and stared gloomily out into the countryside. At least, she assumed it was countryside; it was so pitch-black she could see nothing beyond the far side of the track which wound its lonely way to her left and to her right. Somewhere in the distance a cow mooed mournfully; something cold brushed Kate's cheek, and she realized with a sinking feeling that it had started to snow.

Great, she thought. *Just what I need. When they finally come and get me – if they finally come and get me – I shall be frozen solid. Stuck to the bench. Covered with snow, like icing sugar on a cake.* She sighed heavily and looked at her watch. It was half-past seven.

Mrs Shaddock noticed the movement. 'Not to worry, lovey. I'm sure they won't be long now. I expect there's been some sort of crisis at the school – that's what'll have held them up.'

She spoke reassuringly, but Kate wasn't appeased. *Forty minutes late!* she thought indignantly, self-pity stirring inside her. *They knew my train was due in at ten to, I heard Mr Shaddock tell Aunt Rachel on the phone last night. Why weren't they here to meet me? Why aren't they here now? My parents wouldn't leave me freezing on a rotten old station platform for forty. . . .* Kate remembered suddenly, with such force it made her catch her breath, and she stuffed the

2

thought of her parents to the back of her mind in much the same way as she had stuffed her clothes into her suitcase the night before, until Mrs Shaddock had come into the bedroom which somehow managed to be cold and stuffy at the same time, and had belonged to Mrs Shaddock's daughter until she had got married and left home.

'What's all this?' Mrs Shaddock had exclaimed in mock horror, raising her hands to the heavens as if she were about to burst into song. 'You can't throw all your things in like that, Kathleen love. Whatever will your auntie and uncle think – they'll think I haven't been looking after you properly these last weeks, that's what they'll think. Here, let me,' and she had tipped everything out on to the mustard satin counterpane and begun folding it all up, slowly and carefully. Kate had looked around the bedroom and wondered, not for the first time, what sort of person would deliberately choose to surround herself with so much mustard. She wasn't sorry to leave the Shaddocks, kind though they had undoubtedly been; she hated being called Kathleen.

Suddenly, there was the unmistakable sound of a car – a rather noisy car – drawing up outside the station, and a door slammed loudly.

'Curses!' a man's voice said, and the door slammed again. Then Kate heard footsteps hurrying through the ticket office behind her, and she forced herself not to turn round and look at whoever it was, although she knew it had to be Uncle Nicholas.

It was. 'Kate!' the voice said. 'There you are!' *Where did you think I was going to be*, Kate wanted to

say, *having a little nature ramble in the dark and the snow?*
But she didn't. Instead she turned to her uncle and
looked up at him, deliberately expressionless.

Uncle Nicholas frowned slightly and peered
anxiously into her face. 'It *is* Kate, isn't it?' He
noticed Mrs Shaddock for the first time, standing
in the shadows; she nodded at him, a small almost
unnoticeable movement of her head.

Uncle Nicholas laughed, rather too loudly. 'Of
course it is; that nose and mouth, you're the image
of your mother. . . .' He trailed off uncomfortably,
then laughed again. He sounded embarrassed.
'It's good to see you, Kate; I'm your Uncle Nick.'
He bent to kiss her, but Kate turned away at the
last moment so that the kiss landed on the tip of her
left ear. Uncle Nicholas didn't appear to notice. He
turned to Mrs Shaddock and shook her hand
warmly.

'Nick Greenwood,' he introduced himself. 'I
can't tell you how grateful I am to you for all you've
done. I just feel so awful that we weren't around
sooner to take care of things; if only we'd known,
she could have come to us immediately. . . .' His
voice cracked, and he trailed off again.

Mrs Shaddock pressed his hand. 'Don't blame
yourself, lovey,' she told him, in a low voice. 'I
understand there were problems. Anyway, the
main thing is she'll be with family now. Foster
parents are all very well, but there's nothing beats
proper family. Isn't that right, Kathleen love?' She
raised her voice, but Kate didn't answer. *Family!*
she thought bitterly. *Some family. I've never even seen
them before.*

Uncle Nicholas smiled ruefully, almost as if he

4

could hear her thoughts. 'Absolutely right. It's just – well, never mind.' He seemed to gather himself. 'Anyway, I'm frightfully sorry I'm so late – you must have wondered what on earth had happened to me. Let's get away, shall we? You will come back for some supper, won't you? It's such a filthy night.'

Mrs Shaddock raised her hands in protest. 'No, no,' she said. 'It's very good of you, but I'm going to my goddaughter in Exeter for the night – she's expecting me. I did tell your wife, on the telephone the other evening.'

'So you did; I'd forgotten. Then can I drop you somewhere?'

'That's kind of you, but Frances ordered me a taxi. It's probably here by now – shall we go and see?'

They walked through the ticket office and out into the snow, Uncle Nicholas and Mrs Shaddock making polite conversation, Kate silent. Sure enough, Mrs Shaddock's taxi was waiting there with the inside light on, its driver reading a newspaper. He folded the paper up and opened the door when he saw them approaching. Kate dawdled behind, but she could still hear their parting words.

'If you're sure that's all right,' Uncle Nicholas was saying anxiously. 'It's very good of you to take the trouble to come all this way and not even come back for a bite to eat.'

Mrs Shaddock was kind, but firm. 'Quite sure, thank you. It was no trouble at all.' She lowered her voice, but Kate could still hear what she said. 'I think it's best that Kathleen enters your home by herself. On her own terms, so to speak. Without a chaperon.'

Uncle Nicholas replied, but the wind took his words away. He saw Mrs Shaddock into the cab and closed the door, and then she was gone, driven away into the night.

He turned to Kate. 'Come on then, my deario; let's get you and your worldly goods into the car. Goodness me, you haven't brought much, have you — I thought girls of your age were always loaded down with bits and bobs. Oh, I forgot; the rest of your stuff's being sent on, isn't it? Rachel did tell me, but I somehow expected to see you surrounded by tennis rackets and trunks and whatnot.'

Kate remained silent, but Uncle Nicholas didn't seem to notice. He picked up her suitcase and shepherded her to the car, which was very long, very battered and very muddy, and seemed full of dogs.

'Oh, don't worry about them,' he told Kate, seeing her drawing back from the waving tails and slavering jaws. 'They won't hurt you, will you, boys?' The dogs wagged and panted in unison, and Uncle Nicholas opened the passenger door and ushered Kate in. As he climbed in beside her and slammed his door, Kate's burst open again. 'Curses!' her uncle said. 'Just give it a slam, will you, there's a love.'

Uncle Nicholas let out the clutch with a jerk, and they shot off into the night. One of the dogs climbed over on to the back seat and, stretching forward, laid its whiskery muzzle on Kate's shoulder with a blissful sigh. Kate wanted to push it off but didn't dare in case it bit her, so she sat very still, not daring to move.

'Sorry I was so late,' Uncle Nicholas apologized again, as they sped down lanes made silent by the softly falling snow. 'Only the boys all came back today and the chaos is stupendous. Apparently it's been snowing hard the other side of the Tamar all day, and quite a lot of them had a tricky journey.' He glanced at her. 'Is Jessie bothering you? Just push her off. She won't mind.'

Kate inched forward in her seat until the dog's nose withdrew from her shoulder. Uncle Nicholas rattled on about nothing in particular, and Kate studied him covertly from under her eyelashes. Because it was so dark – velvet-black, without the constant orange glow in the sky you always get in London – Kate couldn't see very much of him, but what she could see didn't impress her overmuch. Wiry sandy hair, tons of freckles, and weird amber eyes like a cat – she knew that much from the dim lighting as they'd walked through the ticket office. An ordinary profile and a sticky-out Adam's apple, with an obviously hand-knitted scarf just below it. Kate looked at the hands on the steering wheel; a lot of bony wrist protruding from cuffs she suspected were frayed. But the hands themselves had long, flexible fingers; *sensitive fingers*, Kate thought. *Musician's fingers.* She shook herself, angrily. *Don't be such a nit*, she told herself crossly. *Of course he's got musician's fingers; he's a musician, isn't he? He'd hardly have plumber's fingers, or bank manager's fingers, or – or fish fingers!*

Uncle Nicholas saw her movement and thought she had shivered. 'Cold?' he asked sympathetic-

7

ally. 'I'm afraid the heating in this old wreck isn't much cop. Never mind; we'll be home soon.'

The car's headlights swept over a road sign – it was the name of a village. BARTON COURTENAY, it read. And then underneath, in smaller letters, WINNER OF BEST-KEPT VILLAGE CONTEST, 1979. Uncle Nicholas drove past several thatched cottages, a pub with its sign swinging in the wind, and a church with its squat Norman tower and lych gate already frosted with snow; if Kate had been in a better mood she would have thought the village pretty. Then the car swung abruptly off the road, down a drive fringed with tall snow-clad trees, and came to halt outside a large three-storeyed square-built house with a pillared front entrance and light blazing from every window.

'Here we are,' said Uncle Nicholas, in a cheerful voice. 'Appleford House. Welcome. Come along in, then, and meet your aunt and cousins.'

Kate's first impression of Appleford House was that she had walked into an ants' nest by mistake. Hordes of boys, small and not so small, swarmed noisily around; they were all dressed identically in dark-grey trousers and bottle-green blazers, and they patted the dogs and greeted Uncle Nicholas as he bore Kate through the entrance hall.

'Hello, Mr Greenwood – evening, Sir – hello, Sir, did you have a nice Christmas, Sir?'

Uncle Nicholas answered them all and seemed to know all their names, which amazed Kate. She felt dizzy with the noise and the bustle and the lights, so bright and glaring after the dark of the railway station and the drive from it. Her uncle opened a large wooden door, and as it swung shut

8

behind them, the boys' din receded into the distance.

'Come on through,' Uncle Nicholas urged her. 'Come and meet the gang.' They walked through another hall – but an ordinary one this time, the sort you would find inside somebody's house, with pictures on the walls and twisted barley-sugar banisters going up the stairs – and went through another door, into the sitting room. A woman with untidy black hair was crouched on the hearth rug in front of the blazing fire, her arm around another green-blazered small boy who was sniffing un-happily.

'Don't worry,' the woman was telling him gently. 'You don't really need your slippers – you can wear socks with your pyjamas in the dorm, and I'll telephone your parents this evening and ask them to put your slippers in the post first thing in the morning. How's that?' The little boy muttered something Kate couldn't hear, and the woman gave him a hug. 'It doesn't matter,' she said. 'Honestly. You'd better go up now, or you'll miss your bath. Off you go now.'

The boy dashed off, wiping his eyes, and the woman clambered to her feet. She caught sight of the two of them standing in the doorway.

'Nicky!' she exclaimed. 'I didn't see you stand-ing there – and this is Kate, yes?'

Kate remained silent.

'This is your Aunt Rachel,' Uncle Nicholas told her. 'Keeping the boys in order, as usual. I expect Kate's hungry. I must go and find matron, and get bathtime sorted out. Where are the troops?'

'Oh, around,' Aunt Rachel said vaguely. She

advanced on Kate and unbuttoned her coat. 'Goodness me, child, you're frozen; take that coat off and go and sit by the fire. I'll bring you some supper: is soup and cheese on toast all right? You can eat that in peace and then you can meet the rest of the family. I thought it would be a bit over-whelming to meet everyone at once.' She put her hand under Kate's chin and raised it so she could look into her eyes. Aunt Rachel's eyes misted over. 'Poor little love,' she said, softly. 'It's all right now. You'll be all right; we'll look after you.' But Kate knew it wasn't all right, it wasn't all right at all. It was all wrong, and it was never going to be all right again.

When she had finished her supper, a tabby cat appeared from nowhere and jumped up on to Kate's lap. She didn't normally like cats, but this one gave her an odd sort of comfort as it lay there, purring ecstatically. Then her cousins filed in silently and stood in front of her; she was suddenly reminded of a photograph she had once seen of the Queen inspecting her troops. She looked down uncomfortably, and picked at a loose thread on her sleeve.

'For heaven's sake, you lot!' exclaimed Aunt Rachel. 'Don't stand there staring at the poor child; she's not a monkey at the zoo!' She crossed the room and sat on the arm of Kate's chair. 'Let me introduce you to my impolite offspring. The beanpole on the end there is Gus – Gus, say hello to your cousin. Gus is frightfully musical, just like his father,' Aunt Rachel said to Kate. 'He's a music scholar at Pevensie College.' This piece of information meant nothing to Kate, but she could tell from the pride in her aunt's voice that she was supposed to be impressed.

The beanpole grinned amiably at her. 'Hello, Kate,' he said.

'Then there's Ned. He's the brains of the family; he's going to be a nuclear physicist when he grows up, or is it a metallurgist? I can never keep up.'

Ned looked very much like Uncle Nicholas, but on him the thick wiry hair was a startlingly bright ginger, and the weird amber eyes were magnified behind round wire-rimmed spectacles. He lifted a hand at Kate.

'Hi,' he said, economically.

Aunt Rachel continued the cousin inventory. 'Next comes Charley – Charley's favourite pastimes are getting muddy and ripping the knees out of perfectly good jeans, but not necessarily in that order.' Charley grinned a huge white grin. 'And on the other end is Harry. He's in love with his teacher.'

'No I'm not!' Harry said hotly. 'Miss Maltby's got a boyfriend – he makes her wear perfume and red lipstick when she goes to see him. But she's not going to marry him – Miss Maltby says . . .'

The whole family groaned. 'See what I mean?' said Aunt Rachel.

Just then the door swung open, and a very small boy in Pooh Bear pyjamas and carrying a chewed-looking teddy came into the room, rubbing his eyes. One of the dogs ambled over and sniffed the child's ear and licked his face, but the child pushed it grumpily away.

'Outaway, Max,' he said crossly. He climbed on

11

to his mother's lap, kicking the tabby cat in the face in the process, and whispered in her ear.

'Boots has had a nightmare?' said Aunt Rachel. 'Poor Boots. D'you think he might be able to go back to sleep if we gave him some warm milk?'

The child nodded. 'Look who's come all the way from London to see you,' his mother said to him. 'It's your cousin Kate – aren't you going to say hello to her?' The little boy shook his head, and buried his face in her front. *Little brat*, Kate thought. 'This is Edward,' Aunt Rachel said to her. 'He's a bit shy.'

'No he's not,' said Harry. 'He's just being silly. Mummy, why doesn't Kate say anything? Is she deaf and a dumbo?'

Everybody laughed except Kate, and even Aunt Rachel smiled. *That's right!* Kate thought furiously. *Go on – laugh at me!* She had noticed that all the Greenwoods, apart from Ned, looked like their mother – the black hair, the great grey black-fringed eyes, the very white skin – and being given the once-over by all these Aunt Rachel lookalikes disconcerted her even more.

'You mean deaf and dumb,' Aunt Rachel corrected him. 'No, of course she's not. I expect she's a bit shy too; after all, meeting you lot for the first time is pretty overwhelming. I don't suppose she's ever seen anything quite like it before, have you, Kate!'

There was a general chorus of 'Oh, Mum!' and the cousins drifted away, saying they had homework to do. Gus said he had to do his packing. Kate wondered where he was going, and then remembered what Aunt Rachel had said about him being a music scholar at Pevensie College. Kate supposed that was his school. *Excuses*, she thought. *They just don't want to have to sit around talking to me, the strange cousin they didn't know existed until a week ago.* Kate was left with Aunt Rachel and Edward; the little boy was sucking his thumb and regarding his cousin with huge eyes. Now she had met all the Greenwoods, she felt even worse than when Mrs Shaddock had first told her she was going to live with them. Four boys and a girl, Mrs Shaddock had said; she had definitely said a girl.

'It'll be lovely, Kathleen,' Mrs Shaddock had told her. 'In Devon, on the edge of Dartmoor – Mr Shaddock and I went to Devon for our honeymoon, isn't that a coincidence! It was lovely. And you'll be living in the school where your uncle teaches, so that'll be your education taken care of. Isn't that lucky? And the little girl is about your age, I believe, so she'll be company for you. It'll be really lovely, Kathleen – just you wait and see.'

Kate had wished Mrs Shaddock would stop calling her Kathleen, and would use a word other than lovely for a change. She had obviously been wrong about there being a girl; Kate had seen with her own eyes that all the Greenwoods were boys.

Aunt Rachel brought Edward his milk and then took him back to bed. Kate dozed in front of the fire; the long day, the wait at the station, meeting all those new people, the food – they were all making her very sleepy. When Aunt Rachel came back, she chivvied Kate off to bed. 'Come on, lovey,' she said. 'You look worn out. I've put you in with Charley – it was a bit of a squeeze, but we managed to get another bed in. You can have half the room each. Oh, and I've put a hot-water bottle in your bed, so mind you don't burn your feet.' Kate hardly heard. *No!* she was yelling inside her head, appalled. *No! You can't put me in with a boy! I can't share a room with a boy!*

But Aunt Rachel hadn't finished. 'Charley's really been looking forward to you coming,' she told Kate. 'She's always wanted a sister; she gets a bit lonely, sometimes, being the only girl amongst all those boys, and the middle one too. I hope you get on well together – I'm sure you'll be great friends.'

So that's it! Kate thought. Charley's *the girl! Good grief, what a mess; that short hair, and those awful clothes – and what was it Aunt Rachel had said about her getting dirty and ripping her jeans?* Kate was convinced they wouldn't get on. Charley wasn't her sort at all.

At last, everybody was in bed. Uncle Nicholas did his rounds of the dormitories and then sat in the kitchen drinking cocoa with Aunt Rachel and the dogs. They suddenly realized Kate hadn't said a word all evening.

'You do think she'll be all right, don't you?' he said anxiously to Aunt Rachel. 'The poor kid looked absolutely shell-shocked when I collected her from the station.'

Aunt Rachel stirred her cocoa thoughtfully. 'Just give her time,' she said. 'I'm sure she'll soon settle down. She's been through such a lot these past few weeks; it's bound to have had some effect on her. We'll all have to do as much as we can to make her feel at home. God knows, it's the only home she's got now, poor little lamb.'

Kate held her breath when her aunt and uncle

crept wordlessly into Charley's bedroom, checking they were both asleep. The light from the landing slanted in through the door and fell across the snoring hump that was Charley. Kate hoped they wouldn't realize she was still awake. When they had gone, she let out her breath in a long shuddering sigh and wiped her tear-stained face on the pillow. *Oh God*, she thought bleakly, *please don't make me stay here. I hate it! I hate it! I hate it!*

2
Charley

Kate was late down to breakfast the next morning. When she woke up, Charley's bed was empty; she didn't know what the time was, or whether to get up or stay put. She lay there in that comfortable doze midway between true sleep and full wakefulness – she didn't know if it was for hours or minutes, but she wanted to delay getting up for as long as possible because that meant she didn't have to face the day ahead.

Suddenly, a bell rang loudly the other side of the wall, making her jump. She'd forgotten she was in a school. It was no good, she couldn't get back to sleep again after *that*. She put her dressing gown on and went downstairs in search of breakfast.

Everybody else was dressed and sitting around the breakfast table. Kate was embarrassed that she was still in her night things.

'Oh,' she said, flushing. 'I'm sorry, I didn't know you were all –'

Aunt Rachel interrupted her, smiling warmly. 'It's all right, lovey. We didn't wake you; I wanted to make sure you had a good night's sleep. *Did* you sleep well?'

Kate nodded, cross with herself for having

started the day with an apology. She hadn't really intended to carry on not speaking to anyone – she realized she couldn't go through the rest of her life ignoring everybody – but she had wanted them all to think that she was coping with things. That way she could almost convince herself that she was. Stumbling down to breakfast late, in her nightie, had put her on the defensive, made her feel caught out. It wouldn't have given the right impression at all.

Strangely, nobody seemed particularly bothered about the impression Kate had made. The room was full of noise – chatter, the kettle boiling, a radio on in the corner – and everybody seemed to be engrossed in breakfast. They had hardly noticed Kate's entrance.

Gus moved his plate of toast and his stool along the table. 'Shove up, Charley,' he told his sister. 'Let Kate sit down.'

Charley did as she was told without missing a mouthful of the porridge she was hungrily spooning down. She looked up at Kate and beamed.

Aunt Rachel put a bowl of porridge down on the table in front of Kate. 'There you are, my dear,' she said. 'You get that inside you. You'll need a warm breakfast today; have you seen the weather? It's been snowing all night.'

Kate looked out of the kitchen window. The snow was heaped up on the window ledge outside, and a black-and-white cat was sitting on the windowsill over the radiator, glaring balefully at the flurry of activity on top of the bird table just outside the window.

Charley followed her gaze. 'It's not the birds he

17

wants,' she explained. 'He knows there's bacon rind out there.'

'Mummee,' said Edward, taking his face out of his mug. He had a milk moustache. 'What's baker rine?'

'It's the hard bits on bacon nobody wants. Come on now, eat up your porridge before it gets cold.'

Edward stuck his bottom lip out. 'Don't like it,' he pronounced.

'You did yesterday,' his mother said, mildly.

'Don't today.' He pushed the bowl, which had rabbits around the rim, into the middle of the table, and settled himself back into his chair. His legs stuck out stiffly. He applied himself to his milk again, and regarded Kate solemnly over the top of his mug.

Kate drizzled golden syrup over the top of her porridge and stuck her spoon into it. She realized she was hungry; she'd only had a few sandwiches on the train yesterday, and then just the light supper when she arrived. She suddenly noticed somebody was missing from the breakfast table, and turned to her aunt.

'Where's Uncle Nicholas?'

'Oh, hooray,' said Ned drily, pushing his glasses up his nose. 'It does converse, then!'

Kate flushed again. Normally she would have said something sarcastic back, but she couldn't seem to think of anything. Aunt Rachel removed Ned's plate and cuffed him gently round the ear.

'Shut up, Ned,' she said evenly. 'There's no call for that sort of comment. You'd better get your things together and go on down; you'll be late for prayers.'

After he had gone, Charley turned anxiously to Kate. 'You mustn't mind Ned,' she said. 'He didn't mean to be rude. It's just – you were so quiet yesterday, we all wondered if you were all right. You *are* all right, aren't you?'

Kate ate another spoonful of porridge while she considered her answer. *Am I all right?* she wondered. *Will I ever be all right again? What is all right, anyway? And why mustn't I mind Ned?*

'Yes,' she said. It seemed easier, somehow. 'Aunt Rachel, where *is* Uncle Nicholas?'

'He's downstairs, of course,' her aunt said. 'He always has breakfast downstairs, with the boys.' She laughed. 'Though I don't know why I expect you to know that, just because it's what we're used to. He's a housemaster, Kate; he has to be around at mealtimes to crack the whip. Leaving me to crack the whip over this lot; Harry, I'm sure there's no egg left in that shell.' She wiped Edward's mouth deftly, and lifted him from the table. 'Finished? Go and brush your teeth, then.'

Harry turned his eggshell upside down in the eggcup and bashed it with his spoon. 'Crack crack!' he yelled with glee. 'Crack crack! Gus, will you build me a snowman this morning?'

'Can't,' his brother said, getting up from the table. 'I've got some packing to do. And I still haven't finished that English essay – old Parker will crucify me. Charley will help you, won't you, Charley?'

'Oh, yes,' Charley said at once. 'And Kate, too!'

Aunt Rachel started to clear the table. 'Good idea,' she said. 'Get you all out from under my feet for the morning. There's always so much to do at the beginning of term; why all the schools in the country have to start at different times beats me.' She stopped suddenly, and turned to Gus. 'And why haven't you finished your essay? You've had the whole of the holidays. . . .' But Gus had fled.

Kate didn't really want to go and help with the snowman. She didn't like snow, and couldn't understand why anybody did; nasty cold wet stuff. She dawdled in the bathroom and took her time over getting dressed, hoping the others would forget and go on out without her. But when she emerged from the bathroom, there stood Charley in jeans and duffel coat, her head encased in a bright red balaclava. She looked exactly like a boy.

'Come on,' she said impatiently. 'I thought you'd gone down the plughole! The others are already out there.'

Aunt Rachel glanced at them as they went through the kitchen. 'You're surely not going out like that?' she said to Kate, frowning. She looked at her niece's fashionable grey suede ankle boots, her short black skirt and her thin zipped jacket. 'You'll catch your death – you'd best put some jeans on, and some thick socks and wellies. And a warm coat and hat, too; and some gloves.'

Kate stood where she was and lifted her chin. 'I haven't got any other coat. Or any wellingtons,' she said. 'I didn't need them in London.'

Charley stared at her. 'Why not? Don't you get snow there?'

'Of course we do,' Kate said haughtily. 'But I never go out and *play* in it. Only little kids do that,' she added.

'But what about walking, going to school, and shopping and things?' If Charley was offended by Kate's remark about little kids, she didn't show it.

'Daddy drives us everywhere. I mean drove. Or we go by the tube. Or bus.' Kate wondered if they had buses in Barton Courtenay; she wouldn't be surprised if they didn't, it had seemed a very remote sort of place.

'Maybe,' Aunt Rachel said, 'but you'll find things a bit different here. This snow could last for weeks; you'll need some warm clothes. Go and put some jeans on, and I'll find you wellies and things. There's an old coat of Ned's around here somewhere. . . .' She started sorting through a great heap of outer garments piled on hooks by the back door.

Kate still stood there. She could vaguely hear the squeals of Harry and Edward, outside in the snow. She wondered why she felt embarrassed about the jeans. 'I haven't got any,' she admitted finally.

'Haven't got any jeans?' said Aunt Rachel. She stopped sorting through the coats, and looked startled. 'Good heavens. Well, never mind. Let me see; you'll have to borrow some of. . . .' She stopped, and looked at the two girls. The problem was obvious. Kate couldn't possibly borrow a pair of Charley's jeans, because she was much too big. Not too tall – they were more or less the same height – but too fat. Charley was slim and Kate was fat; it was as simple as that. Kate went red for the third time that morning.

'Um – not to worry,' Aunt Rachel said. 'I expect Gus has got an old pair he's grown out of. Oh, don't look like that, lovey,' she said, seeing Kate's face. 'It's not your fault my lot are all so skinny; heaven only knows why they are, they eat enough to feed a medium-sized army.'

But Kate wasn't appeased. She knew what Aunt Rachel was really thinking. *You're fat, that's what she's thinking. And Charley. Fat, fat, fat.*

However, once Kate was in the jeans – tightly belted, and turned up several times; fat or not, she still wasn't Gus's size – it didn't seem to matter so much. It was a beautiful winter's morning, the sun sparkling on the crisp and crunchy snow; Kate couldn't help feeling less fed-up than yesterday, although she tried hard not to. After all those weeks of feeling nothing at all, and then the hollow bruised aching as what had happened began to sink in – the aching she had almost succeeded in burying deep within her – after all that non-feeling, it didn't seem right to be feeling almost cheerful again.

They built a fair-sized snowman, and Harry found some stones to make eyes and a mouth.

'Now we need a carrot, for the nose,' Charley said, and sent Edward into the house to fetch one, but when he came back he'd eaten half of it.

'Yergh,' said Harry, pulling a face. 'Fancy eating it all dirty, with the skin still on!'

But Edward wasn't bothered. 'Like carrots,' he said, smacking his lips.

After a bit, Aunt Rachel came out to fetch Edward in for his lunch. 'You three can stay out here for another half an hour, if you like,' she told them.

'Want to stay out too!' Edward cried, but his

mother picked him up and carried him in tucked under her arm, like a bundle, where he kicked his legs and yelled.

Kate was embarrassed by all the fuss, but the others didn't seem to take any notice. They just carried on crumping up the snow to make the snowman's feet.

'Why was Edward yelling like that?' Kate asked them. Charley just shrugged, but Harry turned to her, a solemn look in his grey eyes.

'He's a holy terror,' he informed her seriously. 'Miss Maltby says –'

'No he's not,' Charley interrupted him. 'He's just little, that's all. He'll have stopped once he gets indoors.'

Sure enough, when they all trooped inside for lunch, there was Edward up at the table on two cushions, spooning minced beef and mashed potato messily into his mouth. He smiled sweetly at Kate as she sat down next to him.

'Hello,' he greeted her. Kate smiled stiffly back at him. She never knew what to say to little kids.

After lunch, Aunt Rachel had to go shopping in Exeter. 'Will you two be all right on your own?' she asked the girls. 'I don't like leaving you on your first afternoon, Kate, but I must pick up those curtains. Charley can show you around school, if you like.'

'I'll show her around too, Mummy,' Harry said eagerly. 'I don't want to go shopping.'

''Fraid you have to.' Aunt Rachel was trying to cram a wriggling Edward into a snowsuit. 'Do keep still, Edward; my goodness, this is getting tight! You need new shoes, Harry – you can't possibly go back to school in those scuffed old things. What-ever would your Miss Maltby think?'

Harry started grumbling, but Aunt Rachel took no notice. 'And Gus, don't think you're escaping, either; you seem to have grown about two feet since September. Your school trousers are halfway up your shins – you must have a new pair before you go back.'

Gus shrugged and took an apple from the bowl on the dresser. ''S OK,' he said. 'I don't mind shopping; I wanted to go to Exeter sometime anyway, to spend my Christmas money. I saw this ace shirt in Jolly's . . .'

Charley nudged Kate and grinned. 'He's got a girlfriend,' she whispered. 'He pretends he hasn't, but he has. She's called Petula, isn't that a gross name? This time last year he'd have spent his Christmas money on music, or records of Bach or something.'

'Shut up, Charlotte,' said Gus, going red. 'You don't know what you're talking about.'

'Don't call me Charlotte!' Charley looked cross.

Aunt Rachel finished levering Edward into his outdoor clothes. He looked like the Abominable Snowman, Kate thought; or the Abominable Snowbaby. 'Do stop quarrelling, you two,' Aunt Rachel admonished them. 'Now come along, Harry, or the shops will be shut before we get there.'

It seemed very quiet once they'd all gone.

'Now then,' Charley said as the door shut behind them. 'Would you like the famous Apple-ford House guided tour?'

24

'Not really,' Kate said, but Charley didn't seem to have heard.

'Come on,' she said, leading her cousin through the front door. 'We'll start in the entrance hall – that's where Dad always begins with prospective parents.'

So Charley showed Kate around the school, and despite herself Kate got quite interested. They finished up outside a classroom. Kate could hear the sounds of singing and a piano coming from inside.

'Aren't we going in?' she asked, her hand on the doorknob.

Charley shook her head. 'We can't – Dad's teaching in there.'

'But they're only singing. He wouldn't mind, would he?' At Kate's old school the teacher would have been only too pleased to have had a singing class interrupted.

But Charley was quite firm. 'Yes, he would,' she said, steering Kate away.

'But it's just singing,' Kate persisted. 'It's not an important subject, is it, like English or maths?'

Charley stared at her. 'It's not just singing,' she said. 'It's *music*. Of course it's important!'

She looked quite horrified, as though Kate had sworn in church. Kate knew that Uncle Nicholas was the music teacher at Appleford House, but she had never thought of music as being a proper subject before.

'Do you all play instruments, then?' she asked. She wasn't really interested; it was just something to say.

Charley nodded, and they turned away from the

classroom door and started to walk down the corridor. 'Gus is the best,' she said. 'He's a pianist. He did his Grade Eight two years ago – he wants to be a professional musician when he grows up. He used to sing in the cathedral choir before his voice broke, too; he was head chorister. He got a music scholarship to Pev's – oh, Mum told you that last night, didn't she?' Charley said all this in a very matter-of-fact voice, not sounding as though she was boasting about her brother at all, even though Kate could tell that doing Grade Eight and being head chorister and getting a music scholarship were something pretty special.

'Ned plays the piano too,' Charley continued. 'He's OK, but not as good as Gus. I do the violin, but I'm hopeless. Dad says he doesn't think I'm a string player, but he wants me to stick at it for a while to make sure. And Harry plays the recorder – he can play "Once in Royal David's City" and "God Save the Queen". Edward's too little, and Mum listens to us all. What about you?'

'No,' Kate said loftily. 'I don't do music. I do ballet.'

To Kate's surprise, Charley beamed. '*Do* you? Oh, lucky you; I love ballet. What's your favourite piece? I think mine's the "Waltz of the Flowers" – you know, the *Nutcracker*. Or the *pas-de-deux* from *Swan Lake*; that scrummy violin solo. I just love Tchaikovsky,' and she kissed the air and started to sing in a pure, thin voice.

'I don't know those dances,' Kate said. She'd never heard of Tchaikovsky, either.

'They're not dances, they're bits of music,' Charley said scornfully. She stopped. 'Well, I

26

suppose they are dances, strictly speaking, but I was talking about the music.' Then she peered at Kate. 'Oh, you mean you *do* ballet? You *dance*? Oh, no, I don't like that; it's wet.'

'No it's not!' Kate said hotly. She wasn't having this tomboy cousin of hers showing off about music, and then telling her what *she* did was wet. 'It's very artistic – my teacher says I show great promise.'

'Oh, yes, I'm sure you do,' said Charley hastily. 'I just meant I wouldn't want to do it, that's all.' She sought to change the subject. 'I expect you did lots of fabbo things in London, didn't you? Dad says you can go to two concerts a night for two weeks in London, and not hear the same composer twice.'

'I didn't go to concerts,' Kate said. She was fed up with talking about music. 'I used to go to the museums and things. The art galleries. And to restaurants, quite a bit; my friend Hester had her birthday party in an Italian restaurant in Mayfair. That was quite good. And I used to like going shopping too; I got that skirt I was wearing this morning in Harrods.'

'Did you?' said Charley politely. She'd never heard of Harrods.

'Yes,' Kate went on. 'It cost forty pounds, and that was in the sale. It would have cost sixty-five pounds otherwise, so it was a bargain.'

Charley, who had never had forty pounds spent on her at once, let alone on one thing, goggled at Kate. 'Golly!' she said. 'Are all your clothes that expensive?'

Kate realized she had a captive audience. For the first time since she arrived at Appleford House she felt important, instead of an unwilling outsider. She got into her stride.

'Most of them,' she said. 'Even my school uniform for this year cost over two hundred pounds, with all the extras and everything.' She stopped suddenly, remembering with a pang all the lovely new clothes she'd barely worn, and all the things she would never wear now, like the swimming costume and the tennis dress. Mrs Shaddock had given them – *given* them, not sold them – to the school's second-hand shop. 'Some poor deprived soul may as well get some benefit from them,' she'd sighed, folding jerseys and pleated skirts and games blouses.

Charley was obviously thinking along the same lines. 'Two hundred quid!' she said, with a whistle. 'What a waste, with you not going there any more!' She clapped a hand to her mouth and slid her cousin a sidelong glance. 'Sorry,' she apologized. 'I didn't mean to rub it in – to remind you, I mean. I expect you'll miss it; your friends and everything.'

Kate's animated expression disappeared and was replaced by the blank, sullen look of the previous night.

'Not really.' She shrugged. She didn't tell Charley that she hadn't had any proper friends; not real close sharing-secrets-with friends. Hollyfield Lodge hadn't been that kind of place, somehow. 'Mrs MacReady, she was my teacher, she was a real pain. D'you know who my teacher will be here?'

Charley shook her head. 'Depends what class you're in. If you're in mine it's Mr Penrose. He's very strict, but he's OK.'

'When does school start again? I thought it already had; I thought Uncle Nicholas said everybody came back last night.'

Charley frowned slightly. 'You mean, *this* school? Appleford House? That's right – the boarders came back yesterday and the day kids came back today. St Mary's went back last week – we always go back before Dad and Ned, it's not fair – but I didn't go because I had flu. Then when Mum found out about you coming here, she said I might as well stay off until next week and we can both go back together. She said it might be less strange for you that way – already knowing me, I mean.'

A nasty suspicion was forming in Kate's mind. 'You mean – I'm going to this St Mary's with you?' Charley nodded. 'But I thought – I thought I was coming to school here! I thought that was the whole point of coming to live with you!' She felt somehow cheated, despite not having been over-impressed with Appleford House to date.

But Charley laughed. 'You can't come here, silly! It's a boys' school!'

'But I thought – Mrs Shaddock said . . .' Kate floundered. 'What about St Mary's – is that a girls' school?'

'It's mixed – boys and girls. It's just the local primary school.'

Kate was horrified. 'You mean it's a *state* school? But I've always gone to private schools!' she wailed. Another thought occurred to her. 'Anyway, I don't go to primary school any more; I've been at senior school since September.'

'I don't know anything about that.' Charley

sounded as if she didn't care, either. 'But you're definitely going to St Mary's; Mum and Dad were talking about it only last night. Anyway, it's a very nice school,' she added defensively. 'I've gone there since I was five; so's Harry. It's not that bad, Kate, honestly.'

Kate sniffed. 'I'm sure it's fine for you. It's just not what I'm used to. I'll have to talk to Uncle Nicholas.'

'It won't do any good,' said Charley, cheerfully. 'He can't afford to pay for private schools, not with five of us; six, with you,' she added.

'But what about Gus – and Ned?' Kate demanded. 'He comes here, doesn't he?'

'Scholarships. Gus is musical, and Ned is clever. I'm tone-deaf and dim, so I go to St Mary's. And so do you.'

That's what you think, Kate thought furiously, with clenched teeth. *First I have to come and live with a load of relations I don't even know, and then I'm expected to go to a* state *school!* In her mind she had already condemned St Mary's for being rough and ready and ill-equipped. Her father had always paid for her to go to school. 'You'll have the best education we can afford, Katie darling,' he'd always said. 'It will stand you in good stead for the rest of your life.' Somehow, Kate had always taken that to mean that her parents didn't consider state schools to be good enough for her.

But now it looked as if they would have to be. *No more ballet*, she thought mournfully. *No more tennis either, probably, and no more dry skiing or visits to museums or the zoo. I can't go to that dump! I have to talk to Uncle Nicholas – I'm sure he could afford it really. It's not fair, it's just not fair. They can't make me go there – I shall refuse to go!*

But Kate knew, in her heart of hearts, that she would have no choice.

3
One Big Family

Talking to Uncle Nicholas, as Charley had predicted, did no good at all. He was immovable in his
insistence that Kate should go to St Mary's.

'Sorry, Kate,' he said, scratching his chin.
'There's just no way I can afford to send you away
to school.'

'But it doesn't have to *be* away!' Why couldn't he
see the point? 'I just want to go to a decent school –
not that St Mary's dump!'

Uncle Nicholas's eyebrows rose. 'Aren't you
being a bit hasty? Why not wait until you've given
it a try before judging it.'

'I don't need to; I know what it's going to be like.
And why do I have to go back to primary school? I
don't want to be in with the babies again!'

'Yes, I can see you might not be too keen on that.
But Rachel and I thought it would be less daunting
for you to have two terms at primary school here
before starting at secondary school. You can go to
the village school, you see, with Charley and
Harry; otherwise you'd have to go by bus all by
yourself to Exeter. And you shouldn't find the work
too hard, either. I've had a chat with the authori-
ties, and they can't see any reason why you

shouldn't go straight into the second form next year, when you're a bit more settled here. We thought it would be nicer for you this way.'

Kate didn't think it sounded nice at all. And she had thought of something else since talking to Charley the previous day. 'I wouldn't mind going to Exeter by myself,' she declared. 'Anyway, if I went to private school you wouldn't have to pay for it. I've been thinking; my parents had heaps of money, didn't they?' *Hollyfield Lodge, and ballet lessons, and expensive clothes from Harrods*, Kate thought wistfully. 'Well, what's happened to it all? It must still be around somewhere; why can't it pay for me to go to school?'

Uncle Nicholas sighed. 'There wasn't as much as you might think. Your father had put an awful lot back into his business. And the flat's still on the market; the estate agent said it just wouldn't sell at that price and insisted it be lowered by fifteen thousand. . . .' He stopped, realizing all this was going over his niece's head. 'The fact is, Kate, your parents did leave money – of course they did. And they were careful; they were insured, although that wasn't as much as originally expected either. But your father's solicitor has set up a trust fund for you, for your future. There's enough to take care of day-to-day expenses for now, but not an awful lot more until you're older. Certainly not enough to send you to school. I'm sorry,' he added, and he did look sorry, as if just talking about it had upset him a great deal.

'But I want it now!' Kate burst out. 'It's not fair, it's just not fair!'

'You can't have it now,' Uncle Nicholas said

33

simply. 'I'm sorry, Kate. Anyway, think how the others would feel, all your cousins, if you had loads of money to flash around and they didn't. Now that really wouldn't be fair, would it?'

Why should I care about them? Kate thought sulkily. *They don't care about me.* 'I s'pose not,' she muttered. She felt deflated. All her trump cards had been out-trumped. She changed tack, realizing she wasn't getting anywhere with her uncle. 'It's just – it's not what my parents would have wanted, I know it's not.'

For an instant, she thought she might have gone too far. Uncle Nicholas crouched down beside her and looked into her face. He seemed concerned, and didn't speak for a moment.

'I didn't know Patricia well,' he said eventually. 'She was almost grown-up when I was born, and I was only a little boy when there were all those rows about her marrying your father. I suppose I must have wondered what had happened to her, where she had gone, but Mother never spoke about her and Tony – your father – and I suppose after a while I practically forgot I had a sister.'

Kate knew all about her family history. Her mother had never stopped going on about how evil her own mother was, and how badly she'd been treated when she had married Kate's father. Kate's grandmother had taken against him from the start, and would have nothing more to do with either of them once they were married. She had considered him unsuitable, her mother said, but she never told Kate why. Kate had stopped wondering about it all ages ago. But she didn't know why her uncle was bringing it up now; she couldn't see what it had to do with what school she was to attend.

'I didn't even know she'd had a child,' Uncle Nicholas went on.

Well she did, Kate thought crossly. *Me*.

'She had you quite late, you see – they must have been married, oh, fifteen-odd years. Of course, you must know all this. But I didn't know – I didn't know anything about you, and if Mother did, she certainly never told me. The fact is, it came as a terrible shock when we were told about Patricia and Tony; not only the fact of what had happened to them, but that they had left a child.'

You think you *had a shock! How do you think* I *felt?*

'Where *were* you, anyway?' Kate asked her uncle irritably. 'Why did they take so long to let you know about – about it? I thought I was going to have to stay with Mr and Mrs Shaddock for ever.'

Uncle Nicholas sighed, and stood up. 'I'm sorry. We were away for the holidays; living in school does that to you, it's so hectic in term-time that you can't wait to escape. Were the Shaddocks so awful? They sounded very nice over the phone – very caring.'

Kate shrugged, and didn't answer.

Uncle Nicholas put his hand under her chin and lifted it, very gently, until their eyes met.

'Listen to me. I'm sorry you have to go to St Mary's instead of a private school – although I'm sure you'll find you enjoy it, once you settle in. Maybe it isn't what your parents would have wished for you – you'll probably have to go without quite a few of the things you were used to in London. But I can promise you this.'

He bent his head even lower.

'One thing you won't have to go without is love. We want you here in our family, and we welcome you. We welcome you with open arms, Katie.'

Kate swallowed away the ridiculous lump that had formed in her throat and pulled her head away. Only her father had ever called her Katie.

'I still don't want to go there,' she said, ungraciously.

It was the first Sunday of term; Kate had been at Appleford House for nearly a week, and she was due to start at the dreaded St Mary's the following day. The thought of school had been following her around the past few days, like a wasp in summer bent on stinging, and Kate wondered why it was bothering her so much. It wasn't as if she was thick at school; she had always been near the top of her class at Hollyfield Lodge. *I'll just have to show them*, she thought, turning over in bed to face the wall. The rising bell had gone off on the other side of the wall over an hour ago, and Charley had leapt out of bed in her usual keen way. Kate really didn't want to get up. *I don't want to go to St Mary's, either*, she thought glumly. *Oh well, I'll just have to show them that anything the local yokels can do down here in Dismal Devon, I can do just as well. No – better. Ten times better.*

She closed her eyes again, and was just drifting back off to sleep when the bedroom door burst open.

'Wakey wakey!' Harry's voice yelled. 'Wakey, Katie! Up you getty, risey shiney! Mummy says come and have breakfast, or you'll be late for chapel.'

Kate sat up, clutching the bedclothes to her.

'How dare you come in here without knocking! Get out *this instant*, you horrible little boy!' Even to her ears she sounded like Mrs MacReady, her old teacher, but Harry was unimpressed.

'What's the matter?' he said. 'Charley never minds me coming in here, and it's her bedroom.'

'*And mine!*' Kate yelled. She fumbled for a slipper to throw at him, which missed. 'And I'm not going to chapel, so get out! *Get out!*'

Harry withdrew without haste, and a few moments later the door opened again. Kate threw the other slipper without looking, and pulled the bedclothes over her head.

'I think these are yours,' came Aunt Rachel's muffled voice. Kate popped out from under the bedclothes like a startled mole; Aunt Rachel held the slippers out to her.

'Oh. Sorry,' Kate muttered. 'I thought you were Harry.'

Aunt Rachel laughed. 'Do I look like him? I sent him in to get you up; I'm sorry, it never occurred to me you might mind. I should have realized you're not used to strange young men in your boudoir.' She didn't look very repentant, even so. She patted Kate's legs through the bedclothes. 'Come on then, lovey. Scrambled eggs are in the pan – they won't take a moment. You can get dressed afterwards.'

Kate tutted. 'I told Harry, I'm not going to chapel.'

But Aunt Rachel took no notice. 'Oh, I think you'll find you are,' she said pleasantly, and left the room.

Sure enough, and to Kate's slight surprise, an

hour later she was standing in the Greenwoods'
hall, dressed in her best Laura Ashley pinafore
dress and a coat of Charley's.

'It won't do up,' said Aunt Rachel, pulling it
round Kate, 'but at least it'll keep you warm. It's
perishing in that chapel this time of year.'

The coat was scarlet wool with a black velvet
collar – Kate quite liked it, it went well with her
dress.

'I never liked that coat,' Charley confided. 'It
always looked gross on me. It suits you, though.
You can have it if you like,' she said offhandedly.

'I think we can manage to get Kate a coat of her
own; one that fits, preferably,' said Aunt Rachel,
handing out ten-pence pieces for the collection.
'I'll take you into Exeter after school next week,
OK?'

Kate realized she should say thank you. Instead
she put on her sullen expression and looked down
at her shoes. She didn't want charity.

Uncle Nicholas went on ahead, 'to warm the
organ up,' as he put it, and Ned went dashing off in
his school uniform to join his house; he had to sit
with them for the service. The rest of them slipped
and slid their way out of the back of the school and
along a hedge-lined winding path until they came
to a tiny church. For some reason, Charley had left
it out of her guided tour of the other day, and Kate
was enchanted; in the still cold blue morning,
snow-clad, and with the sound of the organ drifting
and curling through the frosty January air, it
seemed like something from a fairytale.

Kate turned to her aunt, struggling up the path
with Edward in her arms.

'Oh,' she breathed. 'Isn't it *pretty*!'

Aunt Rachel gave Kate a surprised look; her niece's face was rosy with the cold and her eyes were sparkling, and she looked more animated and alive than at any time since she'd arrived. She was usually such a pasty, sad little thing, although that was hardly surprising, given the circumstances of her being there.

'Isn't it,' Aunt Rachel agreed, smiling at Kate and setting Edward down. 'We're very proud of our chapel; it's pre-Reformation, you know, and part of the original manor house. It's full of memorial tablets to whole generations of Pomeroys – that's the family who used to own the house.'

Kate hadn't wanted a history lesson. She turned, and walked into the chapel.

Inside, the cold hit her with a physical force. Harry breathed out with a huff through his mouth; his breath hung there in the air, white and smoky.

'Look!' he whispered. 'I'm a dragon!'

The five of them walked solemnly down the aisle to the back. Uncle Nicholas was playing a slow, meandering tune on the organ, which disguised the clunking sound of their footsteps on the stone flags. The chapel's pews were filled with silent green-blazered boys, and Kate was aware of every single eye on her. Her face burned, and when they reached an empty pew and sat down she opened her hymn book and pretended to look for the hymns, her hair swinging around her face like spaniels' ears, hiding her red cheeks. *What are they all staring at?* she thought furiously. *Haven't they ever seen a girl before?* But she knew that wasn't why they were staring.

The headmaster came in with a swirl of black gown; Uncle Nicholas stopped doodling on the organ and everybody stood up. Then the chaplain came in and announced the first hymn, and Uncle Nicholas struck up again. Aunt Rachel, Charley and Harry all began to sing with great gusto; Edward, in Aunt Rachel's arms, fiddled with his mother's hair and sucked his thumb. Kate shoved her hands into the pockets of her borrowed coat and scowled unseeingly at the back of the neck of the boy in front of her. On the rare occasions that she had been to church with her parents she had always enjoyed singing the hymns, but she wasn't willingly going to take part in anything at Apple-ford House.

After the hymn they all sat down. The chaplain and various boys read things from the Bible, then there was another hymn, then some more things were read out. Kate was bored. She sighed loudly, folded her arms, and slid down and back in the pew so that her bottom was on the very edge of the seat. Her toes just reached the dusty blue hassock under the pew in front, and she amused herself by kicking at it with each foot in turn. Sometimes she missed, but when she made contact a small puff of dust rose into the air. Then someone dug her in the ribs, making her jump. It was Harry; he whispered in Kate's ear.

'Mummy says, are you all right?'

Kate nodded, surprised. Of course she was all right; why shouldn't she be?

Harry whispered again. 'Mummy says, in that case, sit up straight.'

Kate shot a look at her aunt, who frowned and

shook her head slightly. Kate scrambled upright, caught out, a sullen expression on her face. The choir filed out and stood on the two narrow chancel steps; they sang something, but Kate was so furious at having been told off, however mildly, that she barely heard them.

Then the headmaster stood up. He went over to the lectern, took his spectacles from an inside pocket and perched them on his nose. Kate's heart sank. This must mean a sermon. Her previous infrequent visits to church had always been marred by the sermons; Kate was sure more people would go to church if only there were no sermons. She sank back down in the pew again and hunched her shoulders, determined not to listen to what the headmaster had to say.

As it happened, though, she had to listen; was forced to, almost. She didn't to start with – she fiddled with the buttons on her cuffs and twirled a strand of hair around her fingers, until she was aware of Aunt Rachel glaring at her again from the other end of the pew. Then she realized that what the headmaster was saying did, after all, have something to do with her. She stopped fidgeting and sat up, listening.

'Those of you who are new to Appleford House, and there are several of you,' the headmaster was saying, with a welcoming smile, 'will doubtless be feeling rather strange. Out of place, unfamiliar with the routine – homesick, probably.'

A pang went through Kate at this. *Much good feeling homesick will do* me, she thought wistfully. *This is supposed to be my home now.*

'But you will be surprised at how quickly you

settle down. You see, we like to think of Appleford House as being like one big family; not perfect, certainly, or without its ups and downs – every family has those – but appreciating everybody's good points and forgiving their bad, enjoying their successes and commiserating with their failures, and above all, being there; supporting, nurturing, *caring.*' His voice trembled with sincerity, and Kate had a sudden urge to giggle. 'So welcome back, boys, and a particularly big welcome to those of you who are new this term. And there is also somebody else I want to welcome.'

The headmaster's gaze travelled across the rows of boys; when his eyes found Kate's, she shivered with horror. *He wouldn't!* she thought. *He couldn't! Not in front of everybody!*

But he did. He tucked his thumbs into the front of his gown and regarded the school over the top of his spectacles.

'Mr and Mrs Greenwood,' he said gravely, 'have a new addition to their family. Not another baby' – this was greeted with a laugh, mainly from the grown-ups sitting at the back, and Aunt Rachel went pink, but she didn't look cross – 'but Mr Greenwood's niece, Kathleen Burtons. She has come to live with them, so I would like to welcome her to Appleford House on behalf of you all, and hope that she soon comes to think of us as being part of her new family.' He beamed benevolently at her, but Kate was far too embarrassed to notice. For the second time that morning she felt the eyes of the entire school on her, and she went scarlet with mortification.

During the prayers that followed the headmaster's sermon she knelt on the dusty hassock and rested her forehead on the ledge of the pew in front. The smooth polished wood felt cool on her burning flesh; she was grateful for the chance to hide her flaming cheeks. *How* could *he*, she thought feverishly. *He must have known they would all stare at me.* Another thought occurred to her. *And what if any of them want to know* why *I've come to live with Aunt Rachel and Uncle Nicholas – what then? What do I tell them? I can't tell them the truth, I just can't!* Her brain ticked over frenziedly, and when they had sung the last hymn and the chaplain announced that there was to be coffee in the dining room for grown-ups and visitors, her heart sank even further into her boots. *What do I say if anyone asks me?* was all she could think.

In the dining room, Aunt Rachel handed her and Charley glasses of orange squash and chocolate biscuits. Kate took hers without lifting her head, hiding behind her swinging spaniel-ears of hair again, as if it really would make her invisible to people. She just wanted to escape back up to the house, where nobody could corner her.

The chaplain came over and shook her hand. 'Hello, Kathleen,' he said, in a friendly way.

'Kate,' Charley corrected him. 'Nobody calls her Kathleen.'

The chaplain inclined his head. 'I do apologize,' he said gravely. Kate scowled, willing him to go away, but he didn't seem to notice. Instead he smiled. He was quite young, and his eyes twinkled warmly. 'How are you settling in?' he asked Kate. 'Getting to know your way around?' He looked the sort of person it would be easy to confide in, but

Kate resisted. She didn't need to confide in anybody – not *anybody*.

'Yes,' she said grudgingly. 'Thank you.'

Just then, Aunt Rachel and Uncle Nicholas came over with the headmaster. He smiled benignly at Kate and shook her hand. 'Hello, ah, Kathleen. How are you, ah, settling in?'

'Kate,' the chaplain said, as Charley had done. 'She doesn't like "Kathleen".'

Kate ignored the headmaster. She was still cross with him for having made everyone stare at her. But nobody seemed to realize she was cross, which spoilt the effect rather, and made her even crosser.

'Mr Bunson is our headmaster,' Uncle Nicholas said, rather unnecessarily, Kate thought. She still ignored him.

Mr Bunson tried again. 'Have you, ah, ever been to Devon before?' he asked.

Kate maintained a stony silence, which was hard as the headmaster was still holding her hand.

'It's all a bit overwhelming for her,' Aunt Rachel said apologetically. 'She's a bit shy, aren't you, Kate?'

'Ah, yes,' said Mr Bunson, nodding his head wisely. 'Well, that's quite understandable, under the circumstances. After all . . .'

But Kate didn't wait for him to explain the circumstances to all and sundry. She pulled her hand away, turned tail and fled.

4
St Mary's

Charley and Harry ran gleefully along the snowy lane, kicking up drifts of the stuff with their sturdily wellingtoned feet. Kate trudged along behind, sunk in gloom.

It's all very well for them *to be full of the joys of spring,* she thought grumpily. They *know where they're going.* They *know everybody at school.* They've *been going there for years.* They . . .

'Come on, Katie!' Harry called. His voice sounded bright and happy. It irritated Kate. 'You're going to be latey! Katie latey, Katie –'

'Oh, do shut up!' Kate snapped. Harry's face fell, and he and Charley exchanged glances.

'We really ought to step on it a bit, you know.' Charley's voice was anxious. 'You don't want to be late for your first morning, do you?'

'I couldn't care less, actually,' Kate said rudely, and pushed past them. Her cousins stood and looked at her with concern and dismay all over their healthy, open, country faces. Kate fought down a strong desire to slap them both and scream.

'What's wrong, Katie?' Harry asked.

'Nothing's *wrong,*' Kate said testily. *Except I don't want to go to your poxy school. And I don't want to be here,*

45

either – I want to go home and I want my parents . . . The
sudden, unbidden thought brought hot tears to the
back of her eyes, and she turned away to hide them.

'Nothing's wrong,' she repeated unsteadily.
'Just stop calling me Katie, that's all.'

Charley turned to her brother. 'You know that
bird's nest you found last summer, in the hedge?'
Harry nodded. 'D'you think it's still there?'

Harry perked up. 'I dunno – shall I go and see?'
And he was off down the lane, a human snow-
plough in yellow wellies.

'Don't be frightened,' Charley said to Kate, once
Harry was out of earshot. 'About school, I mean. I
know I said Mr Penrose is strict, but that's only
with the naughty ones. If you do your work
properly he's ever so nice, honestly.'

'I'm not frightened!' Kate was scornful. 'Why
should I be?'

'Well, it's just – Mum said – well anyway, *I'd* be
frightened, if it were me going to a brand-new
school. Just a little bit. Even though there's no
need,' Charley added hastily.

'Well, I'm not. I'm not frightened of anything,'
Kate boasted.

Charley persisted. 'What *is* the matter, then?
You don't need to worry about having run off like
that after chapel yesterday; Mum and Dad
explained to Mr Bunson that you're still finding
your feet.'

Kate had a sharp vision of herself, footless,
hopping through the jungle and searching for her
missing appendages with a giant butterfly net. She
didn't answer Charley; nothing had been said on
Sunday about her untimely disappearance from

the dining room, and Kate had assumed that her aunt and uncle's silence signified disapproval. It always had at home, and Kate wasn't about to invite a telling-off by mentioning it – even though she thought, deep down, that she deserved one. In a strange way, Kate would have preferred being told off; as it was, she thought people were making allowances for her, and that made her feel like being even ruder.

'Actually,' Charley went on, earnestly, 'I thought you were really brave, not talking to him. I don't blame you, not after he made everyone turn round and look at you like that.' She whistled. 'Poor you. But I wouldn't have had the nerve to ignore him; he usually gets dead cross if people don't answer him. Even Dad's frightened of him – even Mum,' she added, as if that was more remarkable.

Kate preened ever so slightly. 'Well, *I'm* not frightened of him,' she said defiantly. '*I'm* not frightened of anything. Anyway, I thought you said we'd better hurry up? We'll never get to school if we stand here chatting all morning.'

A large chunk of Kate's fears was realized as soon as she saw St Mary's. It was tiny and old and generally grim-looking; Hollyfield Lodge had been old, too, but pretty, with its rosy brick walls and neat, carefully weeded flowerbeds. There was nothing pretty about St Mary's, and no flowerbeds either; it was dilapidated and grimy, with a small playground at the front and backing directly on to fields, where unkempt sheep stared unblinkingly through the palings at Kate, and chewed disconsolately.

Kate sighed, a heavy, I-thought-as-much sort of sigh, and followed Charley into the building. Harry had already disappeared. 'Gone to see his beloved Miss Maltby,' said Charley, with a grin.

It wasn't as bad inside, Kate had reluctantly to admit to herself. All the lights were on to combat the January gloom, and every available inch of wall space was covered with bright paintings and posters and collages and murals. The headmaster took her to her classroom; everybody stood up as they entered.

'This is Kate Burtons, everyone; she's Charley and Harry Greenwood's cousin,' the headmaster announced. Kate had another moment of chill panic that he would tell them all why she was there, as she had at chapel with Mr Bunson. But he didn't.

'I'm sure you'll all be helpful to her,' he said. And then to Kate, 'This is your teacher, Mr Penrose. I'll be in the office doing *those forms*, Chris, if you need me,' he announced mysteriously, and was gone.

Mr Penrose – Chris, Kate supposed – smiled at her.

'Let's find you a seat,' he said. 'Would you like to sit next to Charley, or do you see enough of her at home?' The class laughed, and Charley grinned, to show she hadn't taken offence, but Mr Penrose noticed Kate frowning, and lowered his voice.

'Don't worry,' he whispered encouragingly, taking her elbow. 'You'll soon settle down. They're a friendly bunch, you'll see.'

Kate took her arm away. 'I'm not worried,' she said loudly. 'It's just ... has Mr Thing – the headmaster – has he brought me to the right class?'

'The right class?' Mr Penrose was puzzled. 'Yes, yes, of course he has. It's all been settled – hasn't anybody explained to you? You'll be coming to this school for the next two terms, until –'

'Yes, I know all that,' Kate interrupted impatiently. 'But they all look so young. I'm sure I should be in a higher class.'

'I'm afraid there is no other class,' Mr Penrose told her. 'This is the top one, and you'll find the ages are rather varied. Peggy over there isn't ten until May, but Miles was eleven in September. And you, of course, must be nearly twelve; or are you twelve already?' Mr Penrose smiled at Kate again, but she didn't smile back. *Go on*, she thought, *tell everybody how old I am; then they'll think I'm thick or something, having to come back to primary school!* But she didn't say anything.

'Come and sit down, now,' he said. 'We're doing some geography.'

Kate was given a desk next to Peggy, the nine-year-old, who was fat and podgy with pink cheeks, and wispy fair hair tied back in a ponytail.

Piggy, Kate thought maliciously. *Fat and pink like a pig – she's even got a pigtail. Peggy the Pig. Oh well, at least I know I'm good at geography.* It had been one of her best subjects at Hollyfield Lodge – she knew most of the capital cities of the world off by heart, and was particularly good at rivers – but it was quite different at St Mary's. It didn't even seem like geography. They all sat around one big table with what Mr Penrose called an Ordnance Survey map, and looked for churches and farms. Kate couldn't see any churches or farms, or anything else for that matter – just a load of squiggly red and yellow lines. She soon got bored, and started looking at her classmates, which didn't take very long; there were only twelve of them, thirteen with her. There had been seventeen in her class at Hollyfield Lodge, and her parents had thought *that* was small; that was one reason they had wanted her to go to a private school, because of the small classes.

Well, I don't think much of this bunch, she thought scornfully. *They don't even know how to do geography properly.*

It was the same after playtime, which Kate spent alone in the toilets, scowling at her reflection in the mirror. Charley came in to find her, an anxious expression on her face, and Kate hurriedly turned on the taps and washed her hands thoroughly.

'I'm all right,' she said sulkily. 'Stop following me around. I just wanted to go to the loo, I s'pose that is allowed? Let me wash my hands in peace; I'll be out in a minute.'

But she didn't go and find Charley and her friends when she had finished. Instead she went and sat back at her desk in the classroom, which seemed much bigger now it was empty.

Mr Penrose came back in just before the bell went. He seemed surprised to find Kate there.

'Hello,' he said. He perched on the edge of Kate's desk and smiled at her. 'Did you get lost? The school's not that big really, not once you get used to it.' His breath smelt faintly of cigarettes and coffee. *Yuck!* Kate thought, and turned her head away.

'No,' she said. 'I didn't want to go outside. It's too cold.'

'Oh,' said Mr Penrose. 'Well, it doesn't matter today, because you're new and you didn't know the rules. But in future you must go out to play at playtime, and get some fresh air; everybody has to.'

Kate turned back to face the teacher. 'Even you?' she asked insolently. For a moment Mr Penrose looked back into Kate's eyes, steadily and without expression. Then, suddenly, he smiled.

'No,' he said, 'not me. Unfair, isn't it? But life's like that; there are those who make the rules and those who have to obey them. And while you're at this school, you belong in the second category.'

Mr Penrose smiled again, pleasantly, but Kate knew she'd been given a warning. Then the bell went, and the rest of the class came swarming back in.

After playtime, they had English. They all had to write an essay on the subject Mr Penrose gave them; Kate had done this loads of times, but the subjects she was used to writing about were things like 'My Summer Holidays' or 'When I am Grown-Up'.

Mr Penrose wrote the title on the blackboard: 'Black and White', it said. *Black and white?* Kate thought, mystified. *What on earth are we supposed to write about that? Aunt Rachel's kitchen floor tiles?* She glanced around at the rest of the class – none of them seemed put out in the least, and most of them were already scribbling away. Even Peggy – *Fat*

Piggy – at her side was writing, head down, frowning with concentration.

What a blooming stupid thing to have to write about! Kate looked down at her piece of paper. *In that case, I shall write something stupid. BLACK IS BLACK AND WHITE IS WHITE*, she wrote, and then in a flash of poetic inspiration, *ONE MEANS DAY AND ONE MEANS NIGHT*. All she could think about now was Aunt Rachel's floor tiles, so *BLACK AND WHITE TILES ON KITCHEN FLOORS* was her next line. Then she was stuck. She scratched her head and bit the end of her pen. *What rhymes with floors? Paws, claws, stores, wars – wars! Got it!* She wrote her final line with a flourish. *IF WE WERE ALL THE SAME COLOUR, THERE WOULD BE NO WARS*.

Done it! She put the lid back on her pen, satisfied, and sat back in her chair with her arms folded for the rest of the time.

After the half-hour was up, Mr Penrose told them all to stop writing.

'Right,' he said. 'You can hand your essays in at the end of the morning, but until then, I'd like to hear some of them. Who'd like to start? Becky?'

At Hollyfield Lodge nobody ever willingly read their work out to the class, and the victim, once picked, would squirm and slide in her chair in an agony of embarrassment. Becky, however, stood up immediately without a trace of embarrassment and read out her essay in a loud confident voice. Kate didn't know if it was any good or not; she switched off at once, looking out of the window at the sheep, who continued to chew placidly. She was brought down to earth again by a dig in the ribs from Peggy.

'What?' she hissed. 'What's the matter?'

'Sir,' Peggy hissed back. 'He's talking to you.'

Sure enough, the teacher was looking at Kate and smiling. 'Go on, Kate,' he said, encouragingly. 'Have a go – don't be shy.'

With a start, Kate realized he wanted her to read out her essay – such as it was. Strangely, it didn't even occur to her to wriggle and squirm in her chair, even though, at Hollyfield Lodge, it was sometimes enough to get you out of having to read your work out. But Kate knew she wasn't being asked, she was being told. With a sinking heart, she stood up and read out her effort.

'Black is black and white is white,' she read. 'One means day and one means night. Black and white tiles on kitchen floors. If we were all the same colour there would be no wars.'

The whole class burst out laughing, and Kate felt her face flame. She looked at the floor, wishing it would open up and swallow her. But to her surprise, Mr Penrose spoke kindly to her once the laughter had died down.

'Actually, that's not at all bad,' he said. 'Don't take any notice of this lot – half of them can't make a rhyme to save their lives.'

But Kate knew the class thought she was a joke, and that stung. *How dare they laugh at me! How dare they! Well, I'll show them – I'll just jolly well show them, just see if I don't!*

After lunch, which Kate ate in silence, they had maths. To her dismay they used a different book from the one she was used to, and it all seemed like a foreign language. Then they read quietly to themselves until the bell went for home time.

At least that's something *I can do,* Kate thought miserably, *read to myself. What sort of a school is this, anyway? Everything's totally different. I'll never fit in here. Never ever ever . . .*

She was silent all the way home. When they got back, Aunt Rachel had tea ready for them, laid out on the kitchen table.

'Come on in by the Aga and get warmed up,' she told them, ladling soup into bowls. 'What have you been doing today, *mes enfants*? Anything exciting?'

'We did all about King Arthur and Sir Winalot,' Harry said excitedly. 'It was dead good. Miss Maltby says . . .'

Aunt Rachel and Charley groaned. 'How was your first day, Kate?' Aunt Rachel asked.

Kate shrugged. 'OK.' *I'm not going to tell her it was awful and I couldn't do any of the work; she'll think I'm pathetic.* 'You might have come with me, though. It was awful, having to walk in all by myself. Just awful.'

Harry stared at her, King Arthur and his knights forgotten. 'But you said you didn't want Mummy to come!' he protested. 'She asked you, and you said –'

'That's enough, Harry,' Aunt Rachel said sharply. She looked into Kate's face. 'Did you really want me to come?' she asked softly. 'I would have done if I'd thought you wanted me there. Only you seemed so positive when I asked you.'

Kate shrugged again, inexplicably cross with

her aunt for being reasonable. She felt as if she was being humoured.

'I survived,' she said, bad-temperedly. 'I want to go and read my book now, if that's all right.' And she shoved her chair back with a squeak and stood up.

'Not in your room,' Aunt Rachel said. 'It's too cold; the radiator's not working properly. Stay in here, or go into the sitting room.' The bedroom felt warm enough to Kate when she went in to fetch her book, but she didn't argue. She went and sat in the sitting room, nose buried determinedly in the book so nobody would talk to her.

Presently, Ned came in, slamming the front door behind him. Kate winced.

' 'Lo, Ma,' he greeted Aunt Rachel. 'What's for tea? I'm starving.' He and Charley came into the sitting room. Ned looked surprised to see Kate there. 'Oh, hello.' He didn't seem to know what to say; he wandered over and looked at Kate's book. 'Oh, are you reading that? We did it a couple of terms ago. Good, isn't it?'

'Well, I'm trying to read it now,' Kate said moodily, 'so if you don't mind I'd like to get on with it.'

Ned put on a stuck-up voice. 'Oh, sor-*ry*,' he said sarcastically. 'Pardon me for breathing.'

Kate turned a page and ignored him studiedly. But Ned's blood was up.

'Bet you were a real bundle of laughs at St Mary's today,' he said nastily. 'Bet they all loved you. Bet –'

Charley interrupted. 'Don't be so horrid, Ned,' she told her brother. 'You're not exactly a bundle of laughs yourself, these days.'

'Who asked you?' Ned asked hotly.

'I didn't,' Kate jumped to her own defence. 'I can fight my own battles, thank you very much. I don't need you to stand up for me, *Charlotte* – or anybody else, for that matter.'

Charley went red and bit her top lip, and Ned laughed manically.

'That's telling you, *Charlotte*,' he said. 'Don't stick up for *her*, she doesn't appreciate it. She –'

'Children, children!' Aunt Rachel was standing in the doorway. 'That's quite enough of that. Kate, make yourself useful, please; Edward needs bathing.'

Kate was horrified. 'But I don't know how – I've never . . .'

'That's all right – Edward knows what to do. There are clean pyjamas on the towel rail. Off you go now, chop chop.' Aunt Rachel was quite insistent, and Kate realized for the second time that day that she had no choice in the matter.

Edward sat in the bath surrounded by bubbles and bath toys. 'Duck,' he said happily, holding one out to Kate. 'Pretty duck.'

Kate's heart was in her mouth, thinking he might slip and fall and drown, and she – *she* – would be to blame. But he didn't. He obligingly opened his mouth for Kate to clean his teeth, and stood up when the water got cold.

'Out now,' he said, holding his arms up. Kate lifted him out and wrapped him in a towel.

'What next?' she asked him.

'Powder,' he said, handing her the container. 'And nappy.' Kate had a nasty moment. 'Nappy?'

she said. 'You don't wear nappies.' Edward lifted his chin. 'I do wees at night,' he said proudly.

'Oh.' But she managed, somehow, and the nappy didn't fall off when the little boy stood up, which she half-expected it to do. When she'd got his pyjamas on, Edward ran off into the sitting room.

'Night-night!' he shouted. 'Night-night Mummy, night-night Daddy, night-night Charley, night-night —'

'Never mind night-night,' Aunt Rachel said, scooping him up and planting a kiss on his black head. 'It's time you were in bed. Who's reading your story tonight? Charley?'

'Kate,' Edward said firmly. 'Kate Kate Kate.'

So Kate did. When she had finished reading Edward's carefully chosen book — a really soppy story, Kate thought, all about some daft dog who kept going out in the rain and getting wet — Edward lay down meekly under his duvet. Then he sprang up. 'Kiss,' he demanded.

Kate hesitated for a moment, and then bent down, offering the little boy her cheek. But he wrapped his arms tightly around her neck, to her surprise, and laid his head on her shoulder. Despite herself, Kate put her arms around his little middle and hugged him back, tentatively at first, then harder. He smelt delicious, all clean from the bath and fragrant with baby powder, and his hair was as soft as down against her cheek. She kissed the top of his head, her lips brushing his soft forehead.

'Night-night,' she whispered. 'Sleep tight.'

Edward sighed blissfully. 'I like you,' he said, so

softly she later wondered if she had imagined it. 'You're nice. Edward likes you.' Then he snuggled down, and closed his eyes for sleep.

5

The Granny Plan

After that, bathing Edward became Kate's regular evening chore. She began to enjoy it, even to look forward to it. She felt she could be herself with Edward; he didn't try to jolly her along as everybody else did, he just accepted her as she was. She didn't even have to talk much – he was quite happy to do the talking for both of them. Sometimes she couldn't understand everything he said, but that was all right too; he didn't usually expect her to answer, just to smile and nod.

She liked the cuddles, too. Her family hadn't been what you'd call a *cuddly* family; in fact, she could hardly remember ever having a proper cuddle with either of her parents. They showed their affection in other ways; praise, and warm encouraging words. But actual physical contact wasn't something they really went in for, as a family – it embarrassed them. *Anyway, I wouldn't have wanted them to be all soppy and sloppy, kissing all the time! Yuck! But it's different with Edward. He's only little. Little kids need lots of hugs. I expect I did too, when I was little.*

Edward was the best part about living at Appleford House – the *only* good part, Kate corrected herself. She had been there six weeks, and things were just as bad as when she arrived. Worse. She thought everyone would have stopped treating her delicately by now, but they hadn't; she just knew people were embarrassed by her, and their embarrassment made her want to say or do something really outrageous, something really dreadfully wicked, in order to shock them into a more honest reaction. She thought that she would always be forgiven, probably, no matter what she might say or do. Oh, she was given looks – 'one of those looks', as her mother might have said – but they were looks of sadness, as if her behaviour upset and disappointed her aunt and uncle, rather than making them furious with her. Not that she saw a great deal of them. Uncle Nicholas was teaching all day, and busy with the boys in the house in the evenings. Aunt Rachel was just busy all the time; doing what, Kate could never quite see. The house always looked a real mess, with dead flowers in vases and saucepans soaking in the sink and piles of laundry lying around everywhere, waiting to be ironed. It wasn't what Kate was used to at all; her home had always been pin-neat. Her mother would tell her off if she so much as left a comic on the coffee table. Still, her aunt's and uncle's busy-ness did at least mean she was left more or less to her own devices, which suited her just fine. *I don't want to be checked up on and organized all the time. I just want to be left alone. That's all. Just jolly well left alone!*

However, Aunt Rachel did find the time to take Kate, by herself, into Exeter after school one day, to buy her the promised new clothes, which pleased her. That is, it pleased her until she saw what type of clothes her aunt had in mind for her. In the shop, a big department store, Kate picked up a pair of designer jeans and then, with a cry of delight, fell upon a hip-length cream gabardine jacket that swung out in flared panels from a fitted yoke.

'Oh, look!' she exclaimed to her aunt. 'Isn't that lovely!'

'Very nice,' Aunt Rachel agreed. 'Just pop into the changing room and slip these on, will you? I think they're about the right size.' And to Kate's horror she held out an ordinary dull boring pair of denims and a navy blue duffel coat.

'I can't wear those!' she said, outraged. 'That coat's the pits! And they're boy's jeans!'

'No they're not,' Aunt Rachel said calmly. 'They're just jeans – boy's or girl's. And a duffel will be much more use to you than that jacket. You need something warm with all this snow around. And think how filthy cream would get with you dragging it to school every day.'

Kate stuck out her bottom lip. 'I don't see what's wrong with these jeans,' she insisted.

'They're twice the price of these, that's what's wrong with them. Now come along, Kate; then we can go and get a coffee and a doughnut before we have to go home.'

Money again, Kate thought sulkily. She dragged her feet and hung her head, and refused the doughnut (although she was sorry later, when she saw all the sticky bright red jam oozing out of Aunt Rachel's), but her aunt didn't seem to notice Kate's sullenness. They drove home, Kate sitting silent and mutinous in the back, with the hated jeans and duffel coat in a carrier bag on the seat beside her.

So far as forgiving Kate's sullenness was concerned, Charley was exactly the same. Even Harry was immediately shushed every time he began to protest about something she said. At weekends, when Gus was home from Pevensie College, he was too full of his girlfriend to take any notice of Kate. *Soppy twit!* Ned was still nasty to her, and Kate was perversely pleased about it. He seemed to be the only one, apart from Edward, who was being honest.

It was the same at school, Mr Penrose being all understanding and kind and helpful, and spending ages explaining things to her. It made Kate feel stupid and thick and ignorant, and she just knew that was how the whole class thought of her. Only, of course, they weren't allowed to say anything like that. Even worse, Peggy seemed to have taken to her; she followed her around at playtime, sat next to her to eat dinner, and was always offering to help her with her work.

'Oi'll help you, Kate,' she would say. She had a strong Devon accent; Kate thought it made her sound simple, although she knew she was actually quite clever, despite being only nine.

The trouble was, the nicer people were to her, and the more they overlooked her sulkiness and rudeness and moodiness and sullenness, the sulkier and ruder and moodier and more sullen she seemed to become. Being understood – being *forgiven* – made her feel nastier, somehow. She didn't want to. She felt ashamed and miserable about her behaviour underneath, but angry on top. Angry at her parents, for leaving her all alone. Angry at people for pussy-footing around her and not understanding how she really felt. But most of all, angry with herself, though she didn't know why. And that made her even angrier.

Kate hadn't had any pocket money since she'd arrived at Appleford House. Her parents had given her ten pounds every week. It sounded a lot, but it wasn't really pocket money, more of an allowance; she'd had to buy things like toothpaste and books and birthday presents out of it, as well as ordinary things. Her parents bought her clothes and shoes, but Kate had had to pay for everything else herself; her parents said it was to teach her the value of money, and she had enjoyed the feeling of adultness and independence it gave her. None of the other girls in her class at Hollyfield Lodge had had to buy their own socks. They probably wouldn't even have known where to get them.

It was socks she needed now – socks, and a card for Aunt Rachel, whose birthday it was on Sunday. She didn't want to have to ask for money; it was humiliating. But she eventually screwed herself up to ask Uncle Nicholas – it had to be Uncle Nicholas, she reasoned, because she could hardly ask Aunt Rachel for money for her own birthday card.

'D'you think I could have some pocket money?' she asked him casually after supper one evening, when Aunt Rachel was out of earshot in the kitchen.

'Pocket money? Sure, how much do you want?'

Uncle Nicholas dug around in his pocket and held a coin out to Kate. 'A pound enough?'

Kate looked at it in disgust. She forced herself to be polite. 'Not really. My socks have got a hole; I need some new ones.'

Uncle Nicholas laughed. 'You don't have to buy your own socks! Give them to Rachel and she'll darn them for you.'

'I think they're a bit past darning.' Kate took her slipper off and held her foot out to her uncle; her heel and toe stuck out at either end.

Uncle Nicholas whistled. 'I see what you mean. Tell Rachel, anyway – she'll get you a new pair. She always sees to that sort of thing.'

'I need some money anyway. I need to buy Aunt Rachel a birthday card.' Kate took a deep breath. 'Couldn't I have regular pocket money, every week? I always did at home. I got used to – to budgeting.' She brought the word out with triumph. Talk of budgeting had always impressed her father.

Uncle Nicholas, however, was less impressed. He just laughed again.

'Budgeting, is it?' He just about split his sides. Kate couldn't see what was so funny; she frowned, and felt herself getting cross. Eventually, he pulled himself together. 'Of course you must have regular pocket money, my deario. You should have asked before. Here you are,' and he held out the pound again.

Kate thought he was teasing her. 'That's no good at all!' she burst out. 'That won't buy anything! How am I supposed to get all the things I need with one rotten pound? It won't even buy a decent birthday card!' She was aware of her cousins' eyes on her, shocked at her outburst, and she suddenly noticed Aunt Rachel standing in the doorway.

Uncle Nicholas wasn't laughing any more. 'How much pocket money did you usually get, Kate?' he asked her gently.

'Ten pounds a week,' she told him. Charley gasped, and Kate rounded on her. 'You needn't sound like that,' she said crossly. 'It's not that much; Annabel Strickland used to get seventy pounds a month!'

'Good for Annabel Strickland,' said Ned drily. 'What's she doing, saving up for a racehorse?'

Kate whirled round. 'And you can shut up, too! It's all right for you . . .' But she couldn't think why it was all right for Ned.

'Kate, Kate. . . .' Aunt Rachel came into the sitting room and put an arm around her shoulders. Kate went stiff. She was so cross she felt hot inside. 'Come and sit down a minute.' Her aunt led her to a sofa; it made Kate feel like a small child, and like a small child she had an almost uncontrollable urge to throw herself down on the carpet and drum her feet in a tantrum.

'Now then,' Aunt Rachel said calmly. 'Getting all angry about things doesn't help at all. It sounds to me as if your ten pounds a week wasn't pocket money as such; it was more like an allowance. Is that right?'

Kate nodded, not trusting herself to speak.

'Well, you won't need an allowance here. You just tell me when you need anything – need it, mind, not just have a fancy for something new –

and I'll do my best to get it for you. And Uncle Nicholas will give you a bit of pocket money each week to buy yourself sweets and so on. How does that sound?'

Kate said nothing. It sounded perfectly dreadful to her, used as she was to being self-sufficient as far as money was concerned. But she still didn't trust herself to speak, knowing that if she did she'd probably burst into tears of frustration and rage. Instead she looked down at her foot, still slipperless, and tried to force her big toe even further through the offending hole in her sock.

'And as far as my birthday is concerned,' Aunt Rachel went on, 'I'm touched you want to give me something. But you mustn't spend your money on me. Why not make a card? We all do, you know.'

'We *all* don't,' came Ned's voice, ironically. 'Gus doesn't. He's got pots of money.'

This goaded Kate into a reply. 'I can't either,' she said sulkily. 'I can't draw. I don't see why I can't carry on having my usual allowance. What about all my parents' money?'

'Because that's not the way we do things,' said Aunt Rachel simply. 'I'm afraid you can't have that money now, and that's that. Uncle Nicholas has already explained that it's for your future; you'll just have to accept what you're told.'

'Children always have to accept what they're told,' Kate said. She wanted to sound calm, like Aunt Rachel, but her voice came out wobbly and whiny. 'They never have any choice. They never have any say in anything; they just have to do what they're *told*.' She took a deep breath and rushed on. 'They have to eat what they're given and go to school where they're told and . . . and live where they're *put*. It's not fair. It's just not *fair*!'

And she stood up and rushed out of the room, her heart thumping in her chest at what she'd just said.

She paused in the hallway, certain that somebody would come after her, whether to comfort her or chastise her, Kate didn't know. But nobody came, and in a strange way that made her feel even worse — disappointed, even. She crept back and listened outside the door. She knew she shouldn't, that people always talked about you once you'd gone, and that they were hardly likely to be saying anything nice about her, but she didn't care. She was beyond caring.

'. . . on earth am I doing wrong?' she heard Aunt Rachel say. She didn't sound calm any more. She sounded upset. *Good*, Kate thought. *Now she knows how I feel*. But she wasn't pleased really.

'Nothing,' came Uncle Nicholas's voice, soothingly. 'You said yourself it would be a long haul, remember?'

Charley murmured something Kate couldn't hear.

'We just have to be patient,' Aunt Rachel said, sighing. 'Patient and tolerant. That means you too, Ned.'

Kate heard Ned's reply quite clearly.

'Well, I think she's a spoilt brat. Ten pounds a week *allowance*! Just who does she think she is? OK, I know she's had a hard time, but she can't play on everyone's sympathy for ever!'

Kate thought she would boil over with fury. *How dare he! How does he know what it's like for me?*

67

'She's not,' said Uncle Nicholas, but even through the door Kate could tell he wasn't convinced. 'She's a good girl really, I'm sure she is. She can't help it.'

Kate had heard enough. She stuffed her fingers in her ears and went and locked herself in the lavatory. That was the trouble. She didn't feel good.

I feel Bad. I am Bad. It's because I'm bad that all this has happened to me – to punish me. And it's because I'm bad that nobody likes me. Ned certainly doesn't; Charley doesn't like me, she feels sorry for me. None of the cousins like me. Aunt Rachel and Uncle Nicholas don't; they don't know what to do with me. And nobody at school does. Peggy only wants to be friends because I'm different; like an animal in the zoo is different. People go along to stare at them, don't they? Well, that's how it is with Peggy. I suppose people are trying to be kind, but I know it's just because they feel sorry for me. Well, I don't want their rotten old pity, I just want them to like me. But they won't, because I'm just too bad*!*

She crouched down on the floor with her arms wrapped tightly around herself and rocked to and fro. If she concentrated hard, very hard, on the pattern of trellised roses on the wallpaper, she could stop the tears from squeezing out. She hardly ever cried, and despised herself for almost giving in now. *I'm as good as any of them*, she repeated to herself, over and over again. *I'm as good as any of them*. The tears nearly started again when she heard Edward calling for her to come and give him his bath, but she stuffed her fingers in her ears again, and when she finally took them out he had stopped. She could hear him next door, splashing around and squealing with glee.

She stayed in the lavatory a very long time. Someone came and rattled the door handle, twice, and called her name coaxingly, but Kate stayed where she was. She was hatching a plan. Into her mind – from nowhere, it seemed – had sprung the idea that she didn't have to stay here in Devon. There was somewhere else she could go and live. Her father had no living relatives – he had been an only child, like her, and his own parents had died years and years ago – but she had forgotten all about her granny; Granny Greenwood, her mother's mother, and Uncle Nicholas's too. The fact that her grandmother hadn't spoken to her mother for over twenty-five years, and very probably was unaware of Kate's existence, didn't seem to matter.

The thought came to her like a bolt from the blue. *I don't have to stay here any more!* The idea was tremendously exciting. *Of course I don't! I can go and live with Granny Greenwood! There'll probably be a big family reunion; when she finds out that Mummy and Daddy are dead she'll forgive whatever it is they're supposed to have done, I just know she will! I expect she'll be really pleased to see me.* Romantic images from some half-remembered film popped into her head; a very old lady, in bed and propped up on pillows, embracing a very young flaxen-haired child. 'My darling granddaughter!' she gasped, overcome with emotion. 'I thought I'd never see the day . . .'

All I have to do is write to her and tell her what's happened, and explain how miserable I am here – I'm sure she'd let me go and stay there. She'd have to, really, wouldn't she? After all, I am her granddaughter.

Kate didn't know how she was going to find

Granny's address without asking Uncle Nicholas, but it didn't matter. She'd find it somehow. She was determined to leave Appleford House, and Granny Greenwood was her only hope.

6
Aunt Rachel's Birthday

That Sunday, it was Aunt Rachel's birthday. Kate, cheered up by her plan to write to Granny Greenwood, had made a birthday card for her aunt; Charley had shown her how, cutting suitable things from old cards and sticking them on to a folded sheet of stiff paper. Kate was quite pleased with the result; it wasn't as good as Charley's, but she had to admit it looked more personal, somehow, than the ones you buy in the shops. It was pretty, too, with bunches of pansies and a little girl in a mobcap; Charley's had a racing car on the front, which Kate didn't think was very appropriate for Aunt Rachel.

'It's a Formula One,' Charley explained, as if that made it suitable. 'Isn't it ace?'

In the end Kate had gone with Uncle Nicholas and Edward to help choose Edward's present for his mother.

''Weeties,' Edward said, pointing to a box of chocolates with a picture of a kitten on the front. 'Like choccies. Mummy like choccies too.'

'What d'you reckon, Kate?' Uncle Nicholas asked her. She was pleased he was seeking her opinion. It made her feel important.

'Oh, yes,' she said. 'Hard centres, too. I expect she'll like those.' Then she thought of something. 'As long as she's not on a diet. My mother used to hate being given chocolates when she was on a diet.'

Uncle Nicholas laughed. 'Rachel on a diet? That'll be the day. She never eats enough as it is. No, I think they'll be just perfect.'

Then they went to the post office, where Kate took out some of her savings and she used them to buy a small crystal vase. It sparkled and glittered in the light when Kate took it out of its box to admire. *I couldn't not buy her a present. That would've been mean. After all, it's not her fault I had to come here. She probably didn't want it any more than I did; I should think she's got enough to think about with her own children and all the boys in Uncle Nicholas's house, without having an extra one landed on her.*

Charley and Harry took Aunt Rachel breakfast in bed as a special treat, and afterwards everyone crowded into the bedroom to watch her opening her presents. She sat up in bed in a white lace-trimmed nightie, her black hair tumbling loose around her shoulders and her grey eyes sparkling with excitement. Edward was tucked up in bed beside her and Gus, home for the weekend, was perched on the edge of the bed with her arm around him. Kate thought that Aunt Rachel looked more like his sister than his mother. She was acting like it too, with squeals of delight at every present she opened.

Then Uncle Nicholas put a large candy-striped box on the bed; Aunt Rachel tore the lid off and scrabbled among layers of foamy tissue paper, and withdrew a violet robe that Kate knew was silk by its shimmering sheen. Aunt Rachel squealed again, and clambered out of bed, nearly treading on one of the dogs who was lying, legs stretched stiffly out as if dead, on the rug beside the bed.

'Oh, Nicky!' Aunt Rachel breathed, pulling the robe on and easing her hair out from inside the neck. 'How gorgeous! How – impractical! It's beautiful.'

'Do you like it?' Uncle Nicholas looked pleased.

'Like it? I love it! Thank you, darling.' And she threw her arms around his neck and kissed him, hard, on the lips.

Gus and Ned cheered and whistled, and Charley and Harry looked at each other and raised their eyes to the ceiling. Kate felt a hot tide of embarrassment flood through her; she folded her arms across her chest and looked away. *How could they, snogging like that in front of everybody?* Her parents had never so much as held hands in public. *They shouldn't. It's not right. It's not – not nice.*

After a moment, Edward got fed up with being left out; he climbed across the bed and stood up, holding his arms out towards his parents.

'Kiss too,' he demanded. 'Kiss too!'

Aunt Rachel laughed, and picked him up. He wrapped his legs around her waist, tight, like a little monkey, and nuzzled his face into her neck.

'Honestly,' said Charley to him, mildly. 'Must you be so yukky? It's bad enough having Mum and Dad doing it, without you joining in. Anyway, you're embarrassing Kate.'

Aunt Rachel laughed again, and sat down on the bed. 'Nothing wrong with a bit of cuddling – it's

73

what makes the world go round. You're not embarrassed, are you, Kate?'

'Of course not,' Kate lied. Not knowing what to do with her hands, she shoved her present towards her aunt. 'Here, this is – this is for you. Happy birthday,' she added quickly.

The smile left Aunt Rachel's face, and she sat down on the bed. She looked almost sad. 'Oh, Kate,' she said softly. 'You shouldn't have.' When she took the paper off and saw the card and the little vase, she said it again. 'You shouldn't have. But I'm glad you did, lovey; it's beautiful. Thank you.' And she put her hand up to Kate's face and kissed her cheek.

Kate was embarrassed again, but mixed in with the embarrassment was another, unfamiliar feeling. She looked down and shuffled her feet.

'That's OK,' she mumbled. 'I thought – you could put flowers in it, or something.' As soon as the words were out she expected Ned to say something sarcastic and clever, but rather to her surprise he didn't say anything.

'That's dead pretty,' Gus said to his mother, picking the vase up and inspecting it. 'All those presents – aren't you lucky!' And he leant over and gave her a kiss.

The unfamiliar, unidentified feeling within Kate grew, and she had a sudden peculiar urge to kiss her aunt's other cheek and give her a hug. *Don't be so wet*, she told herself. *They'll think you've gone mental. You're just feeling happier because you know you probably won't have to stay here much longer – you've found an escape route. That's all.*

Even so, she picked Edward up and hugged him

instead. Edward wriggled and grizzled and wanted to get down, and Kate was sorry she had bothered.

Aunt Rachel sensed her disappointment. 'Don't worry,' she said quickly. 'He's just feeling ratty because there weren't any presents for him. Don't be so grumpy, Edward; it's my birthday, not yours.'

But it was no good. Kate's good mood was ruined.

After chapel, they took a picnic lunch up on to Dartmoor. The whole family piled into the long car, dogs and all, and even though the sun was shining, Aunt Rachel made them all wear coats and hats and scarves and wellies.

'I know it's sunny,' she said in answer to Harry's protests, 'but you can still wrap up warm. There'll be snow on the moors; just you wait and see.'

Kate's heart sank even further at the thought of a picnic in the snow. It struck her as being a particularly silly and uncomfortable way of passing the time. Why couldn't they all go to a nice restaurant for lunch, for heaven's sake?

She sat in the back of the car in her jeans and duffel coat (she had tried to get out of wearing them, but to no avail), wedged in between Gus and Charley. They were playing some silly game that involved making up long words from car registration plates; the dafter the word, the louder the laughter. Kate was getting fed up with all the cackling.

'PCD,' yelled Charley, in Kate's left ear. Kate winced. 'Eight letters or over. Bet you can't do it!'

'Peccadillo,' Gus said smugly. 'That's ten letters. I win.'

Charley was outraged. 'That's not a word! Dad, peddacillo isn't a proper word, is it? Gus, you're cheating!'

Gus was unmoved. 'It's peccadillo, not peddacillo, and it is a proper word, so yah boo sucks.'

'What does it mean then, clever clogs?' Charley was clearly unconvinced.

'I know what it means!' Harry said earnestly from the back row of seats. 'It's a place in London. Peccadillo Circus. Miss Maltby went there last year – she says there's a statue there called Eric.'

Kate couldn't contain herself any longer. 'That's Piccadilly Circus,' she said scornfully. 'And it's Eros, not Eric. Any old fool knows that.'

'It's not!' Harry said hotly. 'It's Eric! Miss Maltby said!'

Kate had lived in London all her life and knew very well what the statue in Piccadilly Circus was called. 'Miss Maltby must be an old fool as well, then.'

Harry went magenta with outrage. 'No she's not! She's dead clever, Miss Maltby is! Anyway, if you're so clever, what *is* a pecca – pedda – what Gus said?'

'She doesn't know,' Ned put in. 'You don't think she knows that, do you?'

Aunt Rachel turned round, her arm on the back of the seat. 'Do you think,' she said pleasantly, 'as it's my birthday, we could have just one day without bickering? Please – just for me!'

Charley looked abashed. 'Sorry, Mum. Do *you* know what it means, or is Gus making it up?'

'I know what it means,' Uncle Nicholas said, slowing down. 'It means a quirk, a foible; something you lot have a-plenty.' He pulled up off the road and parked the car. 'Come on now, all out. Peccadillos and all. Or is it peccadilli?' he mused.

'I knew that's what it meant,' Gus boasted. Kate wasn't so sure. She was still none the wiser. She thought peccadilli was bright yellow pickle.

Edward and Harry went rushing off in a flurry of kicked-up snow to build the inevitable snowman, and Gus produced a football, which he and Ned and Charley proceeded to boot about accompanied by loud yells. Uncle Nicholas lifted the bonnet of the car and surveyed the engine quizzically. Aunt Rachel spread two groundsheets and a blanket on the snow and began unpacking the bags and boxes of food. Kate felt like a spare part. The three dogs leapt around barking manically, and she edged away. She was still nervous of them.

'Shall I help you?' she offered her aunt.

Aunt Rachel straightened up, and smiled. 'That's kind of you, Kate, but you go off and play with the others. Enjoy yourself!'

Fat chance of that, Kate thought to herself. She slunk round the other side of the car, wishing she'd brought her book, but Uncle Nicholas spotted her as he slammed the bonnet down.

'Haven't a clue what's wrong with that,' he said cheerfully, wiping his hands on an oily rag. 'Oh well, it's kept going this long, I dare say it'll carry on a bit longer. Hello, Kate, what's the matter?'

'I'm cold,' she mumbled, trying to slide on to the back seat. 'I thought I'd just sit in here for a bit.'

'Of course you're cold!' Uncle Nicholas exclaimed. 'You're just standing around. You need to move about a bit – get the old circulation going.' He called the others over. 'Come on, you lot – how about a game of Dariuses?'

Dariuses was complicated and silly, a cross between tag and rugby, with a fair amount of snowball fight thrown in for good measure. Kate tried not to get too involved, to stay aloof; but she couldn't help herself, it was such fun. At the end of the game she threw herself down with her cousins on to the blanket, where they all lay puffing and panting.

'Fun?' Aunt Rachel enquired, pouring out hot soup from flasks into mugs.

Kate took one, and looked out over the snow-covered moor. It really did look beautiful; bleak, but beautiful.

'Yes,' she said. 'Why's it called Dariuses?'

Harry looked proud. 'After me; I invented it.'

'Then why isn't it called Harrys?'

Ned took a mouthful of steaming soup. 'Because Darius is his proper name. Anyway, you didn't invent it – Dad did. Heaven knows why he called it after you. He should have called it Twit-features.'

'After you,' Gus said, and Ned clouted him. They rolled around on the blanket, heedless of soup and quiche and sausage rolls, until Aunt Rachel stopped them.

'That's quite enough, you two. Do stop it!'

'But why do you call him Harry?' Kate was still trying to work it out.

Gus sat up. 'Because he couldn't say "Darius" when he was little,' he explained. 'It's all Mum and Dad's fault for lumbering us all with such long names. He called himself 'Arry,' he went on, seeing Kate look even more puzzled.

'But Gus isn't a long name,' she said.

Aunt Rachel came to her rescue. 'Gus is really Augustus,' she told her. Kate could see why he preferred Gus. 'And Ned is Benedict. Then when Charley was born, Nicky and I thought we'd pick a name beginning with C . . .'

'And then Darius, and then Edward.' The penny dropped, and Kate thought what very peculiar names her cousins had. Alphabet names. Alphabet cousins. 'I suppose my name should be Felicity, really,' she said, biting into a ham roll. 'Or Fiona. You know, to carry on the alphabet.'

Everyone laughed, and Kate realized she had made a joke, even if it wasn't a very good one. She blushed, and pretended not to have noticed the laughter, but she was actually quite pleased.

'I always say the next one should be called Fred,' Uncle Nicholas said firmly. 'It's a good, solid name, Fred; you can't mess with it.'

Aunt Rachel pulled a face, and opened a cake tin. 'There's not going to *be* a next one. Five is enough for anybody – six,' she added hastily, glancing over to Kate to see if she minded being temporarily forgotten. 'Cake, anyone?'

Kate took a piece of the white-iced birthday cake, and was surprised to find that she didn't mind. She was warm now, from the hectic game of Dariuses and the oxtail soup, and she was full of good food. The air was so clean and clear she could almost taste it; the sun was shining blithely out of a cloudless blue sky, as though it thought it was July instead of March, and the moor, snow-sifted, looked as pretty and picturesque as a postcard. There were even some ponies grazing opposite them, across the road. Her spirits had lifted enormously since Edward had spurned her cuddles that morning.

I don't mind that Aunt Rachel forgot about me, she thought. *Anyway, I shan't be here much longer. Just as soon as I write to Granny Greenwood; then they'll be back to being five again.*

'This cake's jolly good, Rach,' said Uncle Nicholas, cramming the last piece in. 'Who's coming to see the ponies?'

The dogs were locked in the car, and the whole family trooped across the road. Kate brought up the rear, somewhat nervously; she was scared of horses as well as dogs and cats, and these were wild, after all – you never knew what they might do. But when they reached the small group of ponies, all her fear evaporated.

There were six of them; three adults, two adolescents, and a definite baby. The adults took no notice as they approached but simply moved away and continued to graze, pulling up the short scrubby half-frozen grass with a sound like fabric ripping. The younger ones rolled their eyes and kicked up their hooves, and stood reproachfully a short distance away, flicking their tails crossly. The foal didn't notice them immediately; then he looked up, and Kate fell instantly in love. He had deep brown eyes with the longest eyelashes Kate had ever seen, an unkempt fringe, and impossibly long and slender legs.

'Look, Mummy!' Edward breathed, pointing a stubby finger. 'Baby horsy!'

Aunt Rachel bent down and picked him up. 'It's a foal,' she said softly. 'Isn't he cute?'

'What's his name?'

Ned snorted, quietly. 'Dartmoor ponies don't have names, silly,' he said.

'They do if you want them to,' said Aunt Rachel, kissing Edward's head. 'Shaggy. He's called Shaggy.'

Then Edward got bored and wanted to get down, and the others wandered off for another game of Dariuses, but Kate stayed where she was. After a moment, Shaggy moved a few paces closer, then a few more. Kate held her breath, not daring to move. She wished there was some way she could take him home – *back to Appleford House, I mean* – with her. Then he was there beside her, nuzzling at her pockets.

'Hello, Shaggy,' she said, gently. 'Hello, baby. Aren't you beautiful?' She put out a hand, wanting to stroke the black velvet ears, but the foal jumped back, alarmed. 'It's all right; I'm not going to hurt you.' She realized she still had the remains of her piece of birthday cake in her hand and she held it out, willing the pony to come close again. He smelt the food and stretched his neck, the soft lips closing over the unexpected treat Kate held.

'Don't do that!' Ned's voice rang out, startling both Kate and the foal. She dropped the cake, and the pony skittered off to rejoin his parents. Kate wheeled round to face her cousin, white-faced.

Uncle Nicholas came over, hearing Ned shouting. 'What's wrong, Kate?' he asked her, alarmed at the expression on her face, but she just stared bleakly at Ned.

'She was feeding the ponies, and I told her to stop,' he told his father importantly. 'That's all. I don't know why she's standing there looking like – like Lady Macbeth.'

'I expect you startled her,' Uncle Nicholas said sharply. 'You're not always exactly the soul of tact and discretion, are you?' His voice softened as he turned to his niece. 'It's all right, Kate. Ned didn't mean to frighten you. But he is right; you mustn't feed the ponies – you really mustn't. They get too dependent on visitors, you see, and then in the winter when there aren't any they've forgotten how to feed themselves, and they starve.'

'He's gone,' Kate said hollowly. She felt like crying, and clamped her jaws together to stop herself. Two sheep came over and started to eat the dropped cake; they looked up at Kate with their sweet stupid faces, and she aimed a kick at them.

'Don't do that,' Uncle Nicholas said. 'Come and play Dariuses with us. You enjoyed the last game, didn't you?'

'Don't want to.' Kate heard how childish she sounded, but she didn't care. She felt absurdly disappointed. All she had wanted to do was be alone with the foal, to see if it would let her stroke it, and stupid Ned had to come along and yell and spoil everything. *Everything.* She kicked savagely at a rock instead and stubbed her toe, and used it as an excuse to sit in the car instead of playing stupid Dariuses.

Afterwards, they took Kate to see Buckfast Abbey. The cool white stone reflected the gold of the setting afternoon sun as they arrived; inside, too, the walls were cool and white. It was so quiet, and so peaceful; Kate forgot her annoyance and disappointment, and on an impulse sank to her knees on the royal-blue velvet hassock in front of one of the side altars.

'Look,' Uncle Nicholas whispered, nudging Aunt Rachel. 'Look at Kate.'

Aunt Rachel looked, and was touched. 'She did seem to have a nice day, didn't she?' she whispered back. 'Bless her. Perhaps she's really beginning to settle down now.'

Kate prayed fervently, and the sun sank gently outside the abbey. *Hello, God,* she said inside her head, kneeling at the altar. She wasn't sure what you were supposed to say when you prayed. *Hello, God – it's Kate here. Kate Burtons. I know you don't know me very well – I mean I know I don't talk to you very often – but that will all change, I promise. Just do this for me and I'll come to church every week. Honestly.* She realized, vaguely, that you weren't supposed to bargain with God. *Well, I'll try. I'll be good – really good – and nice to people, and things like that. Only please let me find Granny Greenwood's address. And please, please,* please *let her say I can go and live with her.*

7

Little White Lies

Kate had heard about people having missions in life, and it seemed to her that she now had one. But whereas other people's missions seemed dreadfully worthy, and all to do with what they wanted to do when they grew up – be a nurse, a teacher, even a nun – her mission was to find her grandmother's address. She had no doubt, now, that she would find it; she didn't even doubt that her grandmother would agree to having Kate live with her. *Once she reads my letter, I know she'll say yes. She'll understand how miserable I am here, and she just won't be able to say no.* Her certainty had come since the visit to Buckfast Abbey; the atmosphere had felt so magical and mysterious. She was sure God had been listening to her that day and was about to answer her prayers. She could just feel it.

A week or so after Aunt Rachel's birthday, Charley woke up with a headache and a raging sore throat.

'It looks as if that flu's back again,' Aunt Rachel said, clicking her tongue as she withdrew the thermometer from her daughter's mouth. 'You'd better stay in bed, lambkin; I'll write a note for Kate to give to Mr Penrose.'

She ignored Charley's protests about not being able to miss Mr Penrose's spelling test, and ushered Kate from the bedroom. *Fancy worrying about missing a test!* Kate was incredulous. *I'd love the chance to spend a few days in bed.*

Mr Penrose was late arriving in class that morning, and Kate wondered if he had flu, too.

'D'you think Sir is ill?' she asked Tamzin Holsworthy, who sat behind her.

Tamzin shrugged. 'Dunno,' she said. 'I hope so – then we won't have to have that old test! Can *you* spell "fraternal"?'

'Spell it? – I'd never even heard of it!'

Kate and Tamzin grinned at each other, united in their common hatred of tests. 'Tell you what,' Tamzin said, 'I'll test you at playtime if you'll test me.'

Kate considered. 'OK,' she said slowly. 'But only if you don't laugh when I get them wrong.'

One of the boys strutted across the classroom. It was Miles, the oldest and largest boy in the class. 'What's the matter, Dimwit?' he jeered at Kate. 'Can't you spell either?'

Kate flushed scarlet and turned her head away, and two other boys joined in with the jeers. She supposed she should be getting used to it – these three were always picking on her – but she wasn't.

'Dimwit!'

'Dimwit!'

'Fatty!'

To Kate's surprise, Tamzin banged her hands on her desk and stood up.

'Shut up, Miles!' She sounded cross. 'Leave her alone! You think you're so clever, but you're not –

85

you're just boring!' Kate stared at Tamzin as she sat down again and the three boys melted away, thwarted, muttering their jeers under their breath. 'Don't take any notice of them,' she told Kate assuredly. 'They're just stupid. You're not fat, anyway. That's a really nice skirt you're wearing,' she added. 'You haven't half got some nice clothes, haven't you?'

The skirt was one of Kate's Harrods creations. 'Thanks,' she said awkwardly.

'I was quite surprised when I saw you – you know, when you first came. I noticed your dress then – that red one, remember?' Kate remembered. 'Don't know why I was surprised, though. S'pose I was expecting someone like Charley, being her cousin and all; you know, jumper inside out and grass stains on the jeans!' She laughed, rather guiltily. 'I mean, I like Charley right enough, she's a good laugh, but she doesn't really look like something out of *Vogue*, does she?' She pronounced it *Vo-gew*. 'But you always look really smart.'

Kate was taken aback. 'Thanks,' she said again, the unexpected compliment catching her unawares. She didn't know what made her say what she did next. 'It's a present – from my grandmother.'

'Is it?' Tamzin looked down at the jade corduroy covering Kate's ample knees. It was kind of her to say Kate wasn't fat, but Kate knew she was really. 'It's ever so nice, where did she get it?'

For some reason, Kate didn't want to tell her the truth. She didn't think Harrods would impress Tamzin; it certainly hadn't Charley.

'Abroad,' she lied. 'America – Hollywood.' It was the only place in America she could think of in a hurry.

'Golly.' Tamzin was clearly impressed. 'Why does she live there?'

Kate thought about Hollywood. 'She's an actress,' she improvised wildly. 'She's quite famous, actually.'

Kate was aware of Peggy sitting beside her and drinking in every word, her eyes wide.

'Crikey gor blimey!' she breathed. 'What's her name?'

Kate was flustered. 'I don't suppose you'll have heard of her,' she said, picking her nails. 'It's in America she's famous, not here. Anyway, she's quite old; she's . . .' But the arrival of Mr Penrose stopped her from having to lie any more.

However, her powers of imagination were further tested at playtime, when Tamzin and Peggy and three other girls crowded round her in the playground.

'Go on, Kate, tell them about your grandmother,' Tamzin urged her. 'Donna doesn't believe it.'

By now, Kate had had time to think.

'I don't care if you believe it or not,' she told the disbelieving Donna, tossing her head convincingly. 'But it's true. Her name's Mitzi Monroe.' Her neighbours in London had had a cat called Mitzi, a name which Kate had considered very exotic, and Marilyn Monroe was the only film star she could think of from her grandmother's era.

'Mitzi Monroe?' Donna had yet to be convinced. 'That's a funny name!'

87

Kate had thought of that. 'It's not her real one – it's her stage name. Her real name's Ethel – Ethel Gr—' She just managed to stop herself from saying 'Greenwood', realizing that Granny Greenwood was Charley's grandmother too, and she would have been bound to tell her classmates about this famous relative, had she really existed.

She turned it into a cough. 'Ethel Burtons. That's her real name. She's ever so famous in America – well, she was, when she was younger. She does mostly other things now, you know, commercials.' She was pleased with herself for remembering the Americanism, and it appeared to have done the trick, for Donna and the other two girls were now mirroring Tamzin and Peggy's look of wide-eyed astonishment.

For the rest of playtime, Kate regaled them with tales of her imaginary granny's made-up doings.

'And,' she said, lowering her voice, as the bell rang for them to go in again, 'she wants me to go and live with her. She's written to Aunt Rachel and Uncle Nicholas, asking if I can go.'

'To America?' Peggy's eyes were now as large as saucers. 'Are you going?'

'I don't know. Aunt Rachel and Uncle Nicholas want me to live with them, too, you see.'

All thoughts of Tamzin and her testing each other's spellings had been forgotten, but it didn't matter; by some miracle, Kate scored twenty out of twenty in the test. She checked and rechecked her paper, and finally asked Mr Penrose to check it, even though every word corresponded exactly with the ones the teacher had written on the blackboard.

Mr Penrose handed the paper back to Kate, with a smile. 'All correct,' he told her. 'Well done! And Kate,' he added, as she made to go back to her desk. 'Don't be so hard on yourself. You're quite capable of doing very well in a test. You're not a dimwit, you know.'

As she sat down, Kate stuck her tongue out at Miles, who had only scored seven.

There was roast beef and Yorkshire pudding for lunch, and then banana flan, Kate's favourite, and in the afternoon the class was split into small groups to work on their projects. Kate's was about Buildings, and she was working with Tamzin and Donna; they were really nice to her, not quizzing her about Mitzi Monroe, but just being friendly. After school she raced Harry along the lanes all the way back to Appleford House, to his delight, and they both burst through the kitchen door as Aunt Rachel was putting a cake in the oven for tea.

'Whoa!' she said. She looked at the children's bright eyes and rosy cheeks. 'You look well. Did you have a good day?'

'Mm-hmm. Can I scrape the bowl out?' Kate sat down and applied herself to the scrapings. She suddenly remembered her cousin. 'How's Charley?' she asked.

Aunt Rachel took a tray of buns from the oven and closed the door with her foot. 'Not terribly well, I'm afraid. She's sleeping now. It is flu – she was so feverish this afternoon I had to call the doctor out. We all seem pretty immune to each other's germs, but I hope you won't catch it, sharing her room and everything.' Aunt Rachel started to look harassed; she was obviously trying to work out where else Kate could sleep.

Kate hoped she wouldn't catch it, too – she hated being ill, despite welcoming the time off school – but she was suddenly in such a good mood she seemed to glow. 'Never mind,' she said generously. 'If I get it, I get it. Poor old Charley; I hope she feels better soon.'

Aunt Rachel looked closely at her niece. 'How are things going at school?' she asked. 'Do you feel you're settling down now? Are you making friends?'

Kate shrugged, and put the mixing bowl in the washing-up water. 'I suppose so. It's OK – Tamzin Holsworthy's quite nice.' She didn't want to overdo it; Aunt Rachel might think she really *was* settling down, and she didn't want that. 'Only I've got these awful fractions to do for homework. I don't understand them. I hate maths.'

'Fractions?' Ned came suddenly through the door. 'Did you say fractions? I love 'em! I'll give you a hand, if you like,' he said, offhandedly.

Kate, stunned, could only agree, and by the time her homework was done she found that she did understand fractions after all.

After his bath that evening, Edward wouldn't settle down. He didn't want any of the stories Kate offered to read him.

'Nah,' he said, as she showed him each of his books. 'Nah! Nah!'

'You'd better lie down then.' Kate was getting irritated. 'There aren't any more.'

'Nah! Story, story!' Edward began to wail.

'You're a little pain,' she informed him, and he beamed his agreement. 'I know, I'll make one up for you.' Edward looked interested, so she started before he could begin nah-ing again. 'Once upon a time there was a little girl.'

'What her name?' Edward demanded.

Kate thought. 'Katrina,' she said. 'Her name was Katrina. And she was a very nice little girl, but very sad. And do you know why she was sad?'

Edward shook his head.

'Because she didn't have any mummy or daddy; they had died, you see, and so she was all alone.'

'Was they in Hebben?' Edward wanted to know.

'I expect so.'

'With Baby Jesus?'

'Yes. So Katrina —'

'Why?'

Kate looked at Edward.

'Why what?'

'Why was they in Hebben?'

'Because they had died, and all dead people go to Heaven. Anyway —'

'No they don't.' Edward shook his head. 'Our pussy cat didn't. Our pussy cat went in the ground.'

Kate stared at her cousin. She didn't want to get into an argument about death and Heaven with him. She didn't even want to think about it; she wanted to gloss over it.

'Well, Katrina's mummy and daddy didn't — they went to Heaven,' she said firmly. 'So Katrina was sad because she was all alone and didn't have anywhere to live. She had to go out and live in the forest with the wild animals – the bears, and the wolves, and the . . . the . . .'

'Pussy cats,' Edward put in helpfully.

'Yes, if you like, and the . . .'

'Doggies.'

'Yes, the pussy cats and the doggies, and she had to find her own food and dress in wild animal skins and she was very very unhappy.'

'Did she cry?' Edward wanted to know.

'Oh, no. She never cried, because crying is babyish.'

'I cry.'

'I know you do, but you're only two.'

'How old she?'

Kate considered.

'How old do you think?'

Edward thought about it, his head cocked. 'Five,' he pronounced.

'All right, she was five. Anyway, after ever such a long time, she was in the woods one day when she saw two strangers, a man and a woman, coming towards her. They were smiling at her and holding out their hands. "We are your aunt and uncle," they said to her. "Come and live with us – we will look after you."'

'What their names?'

Kate was waiting for that. 'Oh, I don't know – Aunt Peggy and Uncle Miles. So Katrina went to live with them, and she was happy because she thought they were going to love her and take care of her. But do you know what?'

Edward shook his head, and lay down on the bed.

'They didn't want her at all. When they got her

to their house it was all dark and spooky and in the middle of a big black wood, and they had lots of other children – called Eeny, Meeny, Miny and Mo,' she said quickly, as Edward opened his mouth, 'and the other children all had lovely big rooms and lots of toys, but they shut Katrina up in this tiny little room all by herself with nothing to play with. And they gave her one horrible old dress to wear, and guess what they made her eat?'

''Weeties,' Edward said promptly, and stuck his thumb in his mouth.

'No, not sweeties. Bread and water. That's all she had to eat. Dry bread and water.'

Kate took a deep breath. She was shaking.

'Anyway. One day Katrina was sitting in her dark little room, eating her bread and water off an old dish, and when she had finished she thought she'd give the dish a polish.'

'Why?'

'Shush. She just did. So she took out her handkerchief and gave it a rub, and do you know what happened?'

Edward shook his head obediently, and closed his eyes.

'A fairy appeared in a puff of smoke, only she wasn't an ordinary fairy – that's boring – but a little old lady with grey hair. "Hello, Kate – I mean Katrina," she said. "I am your fairy godmother. I am going to get you out of this awful place, away from your wicked Aunt Peggy and Uncle Miles. You are going to come and live with me, and I am going to take very good care of you." So the fairy godmother waved her magic wand, and there was another puff of smoke, and then Katrina realized she was in another house. But she wasn't wearing her raggy old clothes; she was wearing a beautiful sparkly golden dress.'

Kate began to stroke Edward's hair.

'The room she was in was full of light, and beautiful music was playing, all twinkly and violins, and it made Katrina feel like dancing. So she did. Then she looked around the room and she saw a table, and on the table there was the most wonderful food – roast chicken, and tuna sandwiches, and banana flan, and pizza, and chocolate mousse.' Kate's mouth watered. 'So she ate as much as she could. And when she had finished she looked around the room again, and she saw a little bed in the corner. She lay down, and it was the softest bed she had ever lain on, with silk covers and feather pillows, and she went to sleep. And when she woke up she thought she had been dreaming, but there was her fairy godmother watching her. And do you know what she said?'

Edward didn't answer, and she carried on stroking his hair absentmindedly.

'She said, "Hello, Katrina. It's not a dream, it's real. And I'm going to look after you for ever and ever, and I'm going to love you, and love you, and love you."' Kate's voice grew faint. '"I'm not going to let anyone be nasty to you ever again. You're going to be my own special little girl; you're going to have a very happy life here with me, I can tell you." And she did. There. What do you think of that, Edward?'

She looked down at him. He was fast asleep.

Kate sighed, and stood up. 'You're right. It wasn't a very good story.'

8
Bread and Water

Soon after Aunt Rachel's birthday, Ned was to be
thirteen, and the whole Greenwood household
was buzzing with excitement. Personally, Kate
couldn't keep up with all the birthdays; she
couldn't imagine how the others did, either, with
seven to remember.

'Thirteen's special,' Uncle Nicholas said at
supper one evening. 'The last big one before
twenty-one. You're entering your teens, my lad;
ah, those were the days!' A funny, far-off look came
over his face.

'It's eighteen these days, not twenty-one,' Kate
told her uncle, twirling spaghetti round her
fork.

'What is, my deario?' Uncle Nicholas was
clearly lost in memories of his own teens; Kate was
surprised he could remember that far back.

'The big birthday; when you can vote, and
everything,' Kate told him impatiently. 'What you
were just talking about – you know!'

Ned grunted bad-temperedly. 'I can't see what's
so special about being thirteen.'

'Wish it was me.' Harry looked wistful. 'Then I
could stay up until nine o'clock every night, like

95

you. All the good telly programmes are on after I go to bed. 'S not fair.'

'You don't think I stay up watching *telly*, do you?' Ned rolled his eyes heavenwards with an expression of deep despair, and savagely speared an innocent mushroom. 'Tell him, Dad. Tell him about that little thing called Common Entrance, designed solely to stop me enjoying myself for a year. Tell him about all the prep I'm expected to do every night.'

'Don't exaggerate,' Uncle Nicholas told him mildly. 'Anyone'd think you're the only person in the world to do it.'

'Ah yes,' Ned said darkly, 'but not everyone has the *pressures* I have to put up with.'

Kate flushed, and bent her head over her plate. She knew he meant her; the pressure of having this unknown cousin dumped uninvited into his nice cosy little world.

'What pressures?' Charley scoffed. 'What makes it more difficult for you?'

'Having you as a sister, for a start, Fishface,' Ned retorted, and they fell to bickering.

Charley had told Kate about Common Entrance; how everyone in Ned's year, the final one at Appleford House, had to take this special examination, and how they had to pass it before they could go on to another school. She had told Kate all this one day when Ned was being particularly unpleasant and sour-faced.

'You mustn't mind Ned,' she told her cousin. 'It's just CE; he's not usually as gross as this, but he's got to work really hard. Mum says we've got to make allowances.'

She doesn't seem to be making many allowances, Kate thought, as she listened to the two of them calling each other names while the rest of the family stolidly ate their pudding and ignored them. *And she tells me I mustn't mind him!* She wasn't very keen on Ned at the best of times; he was clearly very clever, but he had a very sharp and spiteful tongue and Kate often seemed to be on the receiving end of it. She didn't believe all that guff about Common Entrance – he obviously just resented her being there. *Well, that makes two of us. And he needn't think I care about his stupid CE, or about him either!*

But even though she disliked Ned, Kate knew it would look very odd if she didn't give him a birthday card, at least. When supper was cleared away, and Ned had shut himself away to do his famous prep in the room he shared with Gus, when he was home, Aunt Rachel got out the box of old cards from the cupboard under the stairs. Charley and Harry sat round the kitchen table and started to sort through them.

'You'll do one too, won't you, Kate?' Charley said anxiously.

'Of course she will,' Aunt Rachel said smoothly. 'That one you made for me was beautiful – really artistic.'

Kate sat down with the others and started looking through the cards for something suitable. She had actually rather enjoyed making Aunt Rachel's card, and had been pleased with the result. Everyone had admired it, too, which had been gratifying, although she suspected they had laid the praise on thick for her benefit.

She picked up a large Christmas card with a

Victorian scene on it like an illustration from a book by Charles Dickens. It was good quality, the card thick and glossy – there was a boy with frizzy ginger hair in the foreground that Kate thought looked a bit like Ned. She opened it to cut out the boy, and what she read inside nearly made her drop it in surprise. It was from her grandmother.

To Nicholas and Rachel and Family, it said in black ink, above a printed *Season's Greetings* in fancy swirling print, and then in the same handwriting, *with all good wishes, Mother*. But it was what was written underneath that made Kate draw in her breath.

Here is my new address, it said, and there, unbelievably, it was, printed in the same swirling print: *Mrs Ethel Greenwood, The Old Rectory, Springlade Lane, Reading, Berkshire*.

Kate held her breath and stared at the card until the words went fuzzy and ran into each other. She half-expected them to disappear altogether, but when her vision cleared there they still were. She couldn't believe it; she just couldn't believe it! *So you were listening at Buckfast Abbey!* she said inside her head. *Thank you – oh, thank you! I really shall be good now, I promise, I –*

'What're you looking at, Kate?' Charley asked her. 'Let's see.'

Kate jumped guiltily, and snapped the card shut. 'Nothing,' she said hurriedly, but her cousin was already leaning across the table with an interested – *nosy* – expression on her face. 'It's – it's this boy,' Kate stammered, half-showing the front of the card to Charley and praying she wouldn't recognize it as having come from their grandmother. 'Don't you think it looks like Ned?'

To Kate's relief, Charley glanced at the card with no sign of recognition as to its sender. 'A bit,' she said, and then went back to her cutting-out, her tongue stuck out slightly with concentration.

I must have it. But how on earth do I get it out of here? Kate knew it would look very suspicious if she just strolled off with the card in her hand. But just then, one of the dogs created a diversion by snatching Harry's cutting-out off the edge of the table, and ran round the kitchen with it clamped between its grinning jaws.

'Let go, Max!' Harry shouted, jumping down and chasing the dog. 'Give it back! Charley, make him give it back! Oh, you've spoiled it, you horrid naughty dog!' Harry's voice climbed to a despairing wail, and his sister got wearily down from the table and tried to prise the dog's jaws apart.

Kate, her heart beating very fast, grabbed her grandmother's card and shoved it into the waistband of her skirt, under her jersey, while her cousins were bent over the dog, trying to make him give up his booty.

'It doesn't look too bad,' she said soothingly to Harry, once the dog had relinquished his handiwork. 'If you just stick something over that chewed bit – look, here's a tree, it'll look just right there. I'll help you, if you like.' Relief and gratitude made her generous; Harry forgot his crossness with Max, smiled his thanks and regaled her with stories of his beloved Miss Maltby.

When they had finished, Kate went into the lavatory and locked the door behind her. She withdrew the card from her waistband, and sat down on the seat to read it again. By now it was curved slightly, from where it had sat pressed against her body. She opened it up and read the words again, hardly daring to believe that she had actually found the address and that she wasn't dreaming. She pinched herself on the arm, and then did it again, harder, just to make sure. No, there she still was, the mahogany of the lavatory seat pressing slightly against the backs of her legs, the card with its Dickensian picture and precious words still clutched firmly in her hand.

She unlocked the door, taking care not to make any telltale click, and crept into her bedroom. She carefully and quietly slid open the second drawer of the dressing table she shared with Charley – Charley had the top drawer, her belongings thrown in in a jumble – and felt around for the stationery she knew was just at the front. She pulled out the writing pad, took one envelope from the top of the packet and shut the drawer. Then she took a pen from the colour-sorted arrangement in a flowerpot on her bedside table, and took the whole lot back into the lavatory, where she locked the door again and sat down on the hard wooden seat.

She balanced the notepad on her knees, printed Appleford House's address in careful capitals in the top righthand corner, as she had been taught, and then began to write. She wrote without a pause, her brow creased with concentration, the words flowing from her pen as if the letter were already composed in her head and just needed writing down – as indeed it was, Kate having had several weeks to think about it.

Dear Granny,

I am your granddaughter Kate Burtons. I am Patsy and Tony's daughter. I will be twelve next month. Now came the hard bit. Kate took a deep breath and wrote very fast, to get it over with. *I am sorry to have to tell you that Patsy and Tony* – she crossed that out, and wrote *Mummy and Daddy* instead – *were killed just before Christmas. They were on a business trip in Switzerland and they had a car accident. I am now living with Uncle Nicholas (your son) and Aunt Rachel at the school in Devon. They are trying to be kind, but they have a lot of their own children, and all the boys in their house, and they don't have much time. They don't understand how I feel. I think they just want me to fit in and not make too much fuss and make life uncomfortable for them.*

I also have to go to this awful School, it's really awful, I can't do the work and they all call me Dimwit, especially Miles. It is not what my parents would want for me. Ned is unkind to me too, I know he's got Common Entrance but he is very nasty at times.

The reason I am writing is to ask if I can come and live with you instead. I am very clean and tidy – just ask Aunt Rachel – and I can cook quite well too, so I would be useful around the house. I don't eat much either, so it wouldn't cost very much, but if you like I could do a paper round and give you what I earn. I am asking you please, please let me come and live with you at The Old Rectory, I can't bear it here at Appleford House much longer.

I hope the weather is nice with you, it is quite nice here, and that you are well. I am, except for catching Edward's cold.

From your loving granddaughter,
KATE

When she had finished writing, Kate put the letter without reading it into the envelope, and copied her grandmother's address on to the front in her best handwriting. Then she sealed the envelope, wondering why she felt something wasn't right. She suddenly realized why – a stamp! She had totally forgotten that she would need a stamp. She didn't have any, and she certainly couldn't ask her aunt or uncle for one – they would be bound to ask who she was writing to. It was Saturday afternoon and the post office was closed, so she couldn't go and buy one until after school on Monday; having waited so long to write the letter she was seized with a feverish urgency to post it *now*, and couldn't bear the thought of having to wait until Monday.

Kate nearly sobbed with frustration. Then, dimly, she remembered her mother receiving a letter, ages ago, that the sender had either forgotten or neglected to stamp. Her mother had grumbled for the whole day at having been expected by the postman to pay extra for the privilege of having the letter delivered, when it hadn't been her mistake, and she didn't even particularly want the letter. It had turned out to be a reminder from the library.

Kate wondered whether Granny Greenwood would similarly grumble at having to pay extra for an unwanted letter from an unknown – *unwanted?* – granddaughter. Then she shook herself angrily. *Don't be so wet. Of course she won't mind – how can she, when she reads the letter?*

She seized her pen, and wrote on the back flap of the envelope: *Sorry about the stamp – I haven't got one. I will pay you when I see you.* Then she unlocked the door and crept back into the bedroom, put the writing pad and pen away, and hid the Christmas card and letter at the bottom of her sock drawer.

The next day was Sunday. Kate was woken very early by the sound of her alarm clock ringing, muffled, from where she had put it under her pillow the previous night. She thrashed around in a panic for a moment, dry-mouthed, not knowing where she or the clock were, or why she was being woken by it, instead of by Aunt Rachel as usual. Then she remembered. Quietly, she slid out of bed, taking care not to wake Charley. Then she picked up the heap of clothes she had left at the foot of the bed and tiptoed into the bathroom to put them on.

When she was dressed, Kate went downstairs and let herself out of the house. She had a nasty moment when she heard the glumping noise her wellingtons made along the hall – the snow had melted now, but it had been raining all week – but nobody came shouting down the stairs, demanding to know where she was going at that time of the morning.

Luckily, the front door of the school was unlocked, so she had no problems there. She walked down the front drive, taking care to stay hidden by the trees, until at last she reached it. Just inside the school grounds, to the right of the gatepost, there was an old-fashioned postbox. Kate took her grandmother's letter from the inside pocket of her anorak. She looked at the address, written in blue Biro in her sloping handwriting, for one last time. Then she pushed the envelope through the slot, and turned and trudged past the dripping trees up the drive.

Kate could hardly wait for the next few days to pass. She knew the letter would go first thing on Monday morning – that meant her grandmother would probably get it on Tuesday, or Wednesday at the latest. *Better say Wednesday, to be on the safe side – specially as it might get held up a bit because of the stamp. I expect she'll write immediately, but if she's busy she might take until Thursday. That means I'll get her letter on Friday or Saturday at the latest. By this time next week, I might be packing to go away for good!*

She spent a lot of time in the lavatory, looking at the Christmas card – she knew the message off by heart now, and the address, every stroke of the elegant black writing – or simply holding it, like a talisman, and dreaming of what life at The Old Rectory would be like. She was beginning to know the trellised flowers of the wallpaper pretty well, too. Aunt Rachel was starting to think her niece had a weak stomach, the amount of time she spent locked in there.

On the Tuesday, early in the morning, Kate woke up in a panic, heart thumping. She had suddenly remembered something she had written in the letter. *I am very clean and tidy – just ask Aunt Rachel.* What if Granny did? What if she wrote, or – worse still – telephoned, to ask just that? Kate could just imagine her saying: 'Kate has written to ask if she can come and live with me.' She didn't want that, not at all. For the second time that week, Kate wrote a secret letter in the lavatory.

Dear Granny,

This is just to say, please don't tell Uncle Nicholas and Aunt Rachel I have written to you. It's just that they might be cross if they knew. I think it would be better if you wrote to me asking me to come and live with you, and not mention my letter, if you think that's all right.

I hope the weather is nice, and you are well.

With best wishes,

KATE

By now she had managed to go to the post office and buy some stamps; she put one on the envelope and one inside it, and added a PS to her letter: *I am enclosing a stamp to pay you back for the last letter.* Then she sneaked out to the postbox again, and posted it. She felt much better after that.

Kate felt almost happy at school over the next few days. It was the thought of not having to put up with it for much longer. Charley was over her flu now, but still wasn't back at school, and that gave Kate the opportunity to regale her classmates with even more stories about the glorious life of the famous Mitzi Monroe. She did think she'd gone a bit far when she told them all about the wonderful house her grandmother lived in, particularly when she explained about the solid gold taps in the bathroom: 'one for hot water, one for cold, and one for champagne'. But they didn't bat an eyelid, just sat there goggle-eyed and totally believing.

On Friday, Kate was slightly disappointed at not receiving a letter from Granny Greenwood. She had lurked around in the school entrance hall until the postman's dark shape loomed up outside and dropped a whole host of letters into the wire basket below the letterbox; she picked them up and shuffled through them all quickly, and then more slowly, but it was no good. There was no letter for her addressed in that familiar black handwriting.

At school that morning, she was quieter than usual.

'What's up, Kate?' Tamzin asked her at play-time. 'What's the matter?' She put her hand down to touch Kate's wrist, and her eyes widened. 'What have you done to your arm?'

Kate glanced down, and saw a black bruise blossoming between her elbow and wrist. Edward had done it the previous night – he had slipped when he was getting out of the bath, and grabbed his cousin's arm to stop himself falling. It hadn't hurt much at the time, Kate had been too concerned with saving the little boy, and she was surprised at how dramatic it looked.

Even so, she didn't know what made her say what she did; it just seemed to come out.

'Oh, that,' she said, offhandedly. 'That's noth-ing. You should see the one on my leg.'

Tamzin frowned. 'How did you do it?'

'I – I can't tell you.' Kate lowered her voice, and looked anxiously around. 'Honestly. I just can't, OK?'

'Why not?' Tamzin was beginning to look quite concerned. 'You can tell me, Kate. I won't tell anyone else, I promise.'

Kate looked around again. 'Well – all right. If you promise. Uncle Nicholas did it.' She was surprised at herself for coming out with such a dreadful lie, but was even more surprised at the effect the statement had on Tamzin, who looked at her with horror.

'What?' she gasped. 'Charley's dad? But why?'

Kate shrugged. 'They don't like me.'

'But why not?' Tamzin began to look suspicious. 'I thought you said they wanted you to live with them?'

'That's because they get lots of money for looking after me,' Kate said hastily. 'They still don't like me. When I do something they don't like, they hit me and lock me in my room with bread and water. Just dry bread and water,' she repeated, unconsciously echoing the story she had told Edward.

She examined the bruise on her arm with detached interest, and Tamzin's suspicious look faded. 'Oh,' she said. 'But you must tell someone, Kate. You really must. Why don't you tell Mr Penrose? I'm sure he'd be able to help you.'

The only way she could get Tamzin to shut up about it was to assure her that she would tell Mr Penrose. Kate started to feel uneasy about the lie she had told – uneasy, and guilty. She knew it had been very wrong of her. But she told herself that, as she wasn't going to be there much longer, it didn't matter. Not really.

9

The Liszt Sonata

It was almost Easter. Kate was surprised at how quickly the time had gone since she'd first arrived at Appleford House on that snowy January evening; it had seemed to be dragging, but here she was, nearly three months later. *It's weird. I feel as if I've been here for ever; my London life seems so far away now. I suppose that must mean I'm getting used to it.* The thought alarmed her. *Does that mean I'm starting to forget about Mummy and Daddy? I couldn't – I couldn't!* It seemed disloyal to her parents that the first raw wounds of grief and shock were beginning to heal over, and that she no longer spent every minute of every day hating her life in Devon and refusing to accept it. Not that she *had* accepted it, of course, because she was going to live with Granny Greenwood, just as soon as she wrote to invite her.

The trouble was, she still hadn't heard from her. It was now two weeks since Kate had written, and Granny hadn't replied yet. *I expect she's just got a lot of arrangements to make*, Kate told herself firmly. *She probably didn't have a room ready for me, or anything. I'm sure I'll hear from her soon.* Even so, Kate wrote two more letters over the next two days, repeating how unhappy and miserable she was and begging

Granny Greenwood to write back soon. She crept out to post them in the old postbox at the end of the drive. She was becoming quite fond of that postbox; it seemed to her to have special properties, to be almost like a magic carpet, with its power to take her away from her misery and unhappiness.

One evening during the last week of term, Uncle Nicholas finished writing the last of his school reports and screwed the top back on his pen, with a sigh.

'At last,' he said. 'Now all I have to do is sort them out . . .'

'And give them out, and wait for the inevitable excuses.' Aunt Rachel sounded cross, which was unlike her. She was darning socks – School House socks – and she bit off the thread with an irritable snap. 'How I hate the run-up to the end of term; so much to do to send them back to their mummies all spick and span, and so little time to do it in. Oh damn!' She had stabbed herself with the darning needle, and a bright bauble of blood blossomed on her thumb.

Kate and Charley exchanged glances, and Uncle Nicholas leapt across to his wife, all concern, and wrapped an oversized ink-stained handkerchief around her injured hand.

'Sweetheart,' he said anxiously, 'are you all right? Let me see.' He inspected the damage and was reassured that Aunt Rachel wasn't in danger of needing an immediate blood transfusion. 'Don't do any more, Rach; let them take holey socks back. I'm sure they won't even notice. Don't get angry about it. I've never known you be like this before.'

Aunt Rachel sighed and rested her head against Uncle Nicholas's shoulder, her eyes closed.

'I'm sorry,' she said. 'I expect I'm just tired. There seems to be so much more to do than usual, that's all.'

Uncle Nicholas kissed her forehead. 'I know. It's been a hard term.'

Because of me, they mean. Aunt Rachel kissed Uncle Nicholas back, and Kate grew hot. *I do wish they wouldn't* canoodle *in front of everyone like that. It's so – so unnecessary!* She looked across at Charley – the only other person in the room, as Edward and Harry were in bed and Ned was off in his room doing the inevitable prep. Charley was buried in a book about the FA Cup, and seemed totally oblivious.

'What you need,' Uncle Nicholas went on, getting off the arm of Aunt Rachel's chair, 'is a holiday.'

That brought Charley to life. 'Oh, yes!' she exclaimed, forgetting about Liverpool and Spurs and the rest. 'Where shall we go?'

'A holiday would be wonderful,' Aunt Rachel admitted, 'but we can't afford one. Not after being away for practically the whole of the Christmas holidays.'

'We can afford this one.' Uncle Nicholas's amber cat-eyes began to glow behind his spectacles. 'Peter Cartwright's father has offered us their cottage in Wales for a couple of weeks. They're off to Geneva for Easter, so it's ours if we want it.'

'I've been to Geneva.' Kate hadn't meant to say it; it just popped out. The others stared at her.

'Have you, lovey?' Aunt Rachel said, interested. 'Did you have a wonderful time?'

Kate thought about it – a business trip of her parents', so long ago she could hardly remember, apart from drinking chocolate milk in front of a vast smooth blue lake, and the smooth bored face of the *au pair* who had been hired to look after her, who spoke a funny language Kate couldn't understand. A sudden sharp memory came back to her, like a scene from a film; Kate getting lost in a shop that sold cow bells and cuckoo clocks, and crying for her mummy and refusing to go with Mathilde when she eventually materialized, and Mathilde reasoning and then pleading and then shouting, and later telling Kate's parents she couldn't look after her any more. Her mother had been very cross with Mathilde, Kate remembered, and told her to go at once; then she sat with Kate on her lap and comforted her and told her there would be no more *au pairs* ever again. Kate remembered feeling as though her mother had saved her from a wicked monster, like in a fairytale.

Holidays had been better after that. Her father had gone on business trips by himself, or occasionally her mother had gone, and that had been even better; her father had looked after her then, and they had eaten all their meals in restaurants and Kate had been allowed to stay up late every night. 'Just don't tell your mother,' Daddy would always say, laughing, and Kate had felt as though they shared deliciously illicit secrets.

Their proper holidays had been spent in places with exotic-sounding names like Bali and Gstaad; once, only once, Kate had gone very reluctantly by herself to an activity camp in Littlehampton.

'You'll love it once you're there, Katie,' her father had said, looking at her white and anxious face.

'You'll make lots of friends, darling,' her mother had said. But she hadn't. She had hated every moment, and she never went to another.

Charley wasn't interested in Geneva. 'Oh, let's go to Wales!' she said, looking excited. 'Please say we can go, Mum!'

'It depends,' Aunt Rachel replied. She looked doubtful.

But Uncle Nicholas had already decided. 'Well, actually,' he admitted, sheepishly, 'I've already told Mr Cartwright we'll take it! Besides, it'll do us all good; we could all use a break, I'm sure. Have you ever been to Wales, Kate?'

'No.' Kate had never been to Wales, and she had no desire to go. She had a vague picture in her mind of coal mines and leeks; and sheep. Lots and lots of sheep. She hated sheep.

Aunt Rachel folded the darned socks up and put her sewing basket away.

'It sounds like a *fait accompli*,' she said, smiling faintly. Kate didn't know what a *fait accompli* was, but Aunt Rachel didn't seem to mind, whatever it was. 'When do we go?'

Just then, Ned came into the room. 'Go where?'

'To Wales, darling. Dad's arranged to borrow Peter Cartwright's parents' cottage. He thinks I need a rest. Actually, I quite like the idea; I shall lie on a hammock in the garden and be fed peeled grapes, and do absolutely nothing.'

Uncle Nicholas smiled fondly at her, but Ned

scowled. 'What do we want to go to *Wales* for?' he demanded. 'I can't possibly go, I've got far too much work to do. I shall stay here.'

'I'll stay here too.' Kate didn't really fancy the idea of two weeks with just Ned for company, but she was sure Granny would write soon, any day now, inviting her to go and live with her. She couldn't possibly go away for two weeks; the suspense of wondering whether there would be a letter waiting for her when she got back would kill her. Besides, she just didn't relish the prospect of a bracing family holiday in Wales, having to pretend to enjoy herself.

But Aunt Rachel took no notice. 'Don't be daft,' she told them mildly. 'You can't stay here by yourselves. A break will do both of you the world of good, too. Besides,' she looked at Kate and smiled, 'it'll be your birthday. We'll have to do something special, to celebrate.'

Kate didn't reply. But although she pretended not to care, she was secretly gratified that they had remembered.

One evening at the very end of term, Uncle Nicholas and Aunt Rachel drove Ned, Charley and Kate over to Pevensie College, Gus's school. Gus was playing in a concert. Kate didn't want to go – it seemed an awfully long way to drive just for a boring old school concert – but for once she didn't like to say anything: everybody was acting as if it was a tremendous treat.

They were taking Gus home with them after the concert, so when they arrived at Pevensie College Uncle Nicholas loaded his trunk into the car and

Aunt Rachel fussed around him, straightening his tie and brushing down the shoulders of the crimson blazer Kate had seen him wear when he came home for the weekend. Gus looked embarrassed and wriggled away; a girl with straight shoulder-length hair the colour of a polished conker detached herself from the shadows and threaded her arm through his, and they both wandered off down the corridor.

'Petula,' Charley whispered to Kate. 'Isn't it gross?'

Kate privately thought them both very rude just to go off like that, without saying a word, but nobody else seemed to think it at all odd.

Presently, they all filed solemnly into a large hall. It was quite unlike any other school hall Kate had been in; the floor sloped down slightly towards the large, velvet-curtained stage, and the seats were covered in crimson plush and tipped up, like cinema seats. Kate, despite herself, was impressed.

Uncle Nicholas handed her a programme. *End of Term Concert*, it proclaimed. *Friday 31 March, in the Theatre*. The theatre! Kate was even more impressed.

She was less impressed when the concert started. In fact, she was bored stiff, as what seemed like an endless procession of crimson-blazered boys and girls trooped on and off the stage to polite applause, scraping or squeaking or singing or reciting; she felt cross-eyed with the tedium of it all. She did brighten slightly when, in the middle of Petula's long and complicated-sounding flute solo (*Debussy – Syrinx*, the programme informed her), the school bell suddenly and insistently started to

114

ring. But Petula didn't turn a hair, just carried on playing, even though nobody could hear a note for several seconds. Kate turned to Charley, grinning, but her cousin's eyes were fixed firmly on the stage. *What is the matter with everybody? Surely I can't be the only one who finds all this stuff deadly dull?* But apparently she was, as everybody else seemed as interested in the proceedings as Charley was.

At last, it was Gus's turn. A tall, fair-haired man – the music teacher, Kate supposed – came on to the stage first, to lift the lid of the shiny black grand piano. Kate looked at the programme once more. *Liszt – Sonata in B minor, played by Augustus Greenwood.* It looked wrong. Kate could never think of him as an Augustus.

When Gus himself came onstage, Kate could sense something was different. The clapping that greeted him was louder, more enthusiastic; he *looked* different from the others, more at ease, more – more professional. He sat down on the piano stool and flicked his school blazer out from underneath him, like a concert pianist Kate had once seen on TV, only he had been wearing a tail coat. She was surprised to see Gus had no music; none of the others had played from memory. She hoped Gus wasn't going to forget how the piece went, halfway through; *I would just die of embarrassment. I am his cousin, after all.*

But she needn't have worried. As soon as Gus started to play, Kate was transfixed. She realized there was no danger of his forgetting the music – he was totally bound up in it. It almost seemed as if he was making it up as he went along; it seemed to flow out of him, along his fingers and on to the keys.

Kate was stunned at how *powerfully* her cousin played; tall, thin, dreamy Gus, hammering away at the instrument as if his life depended on it.

And the music itself! It was a long piece, but Kate wasn't bored, not for a second. It changed all the time – dramatic and stormy one minute, tender and romantic the next. She had never heard anything like it. She never wanted it to stop.

When it did stop, when Gus finished playing, there was a moment's utter silence before the applause began. There was nothing remotely polite about it this time; people were cheering and stamping their feet and standing up, and Gus stood up from the piano and bowed, looking exhausted and stunned.

Kate felt stunned too. She realized she had been holding her breath, and she felt the goose pimples standing out on her arms. She couldn't clap, she didn't feel like clapping. If anything, she felt like crying. She felt as if hearing that one piece of music had changed her life.

Eventually, she stole a glance at her aunt and uncle. They were clapping hard, and looking very proud. Kate realized with a start that she was proud, too, although she would never have admitted it to anyone.

Afterwards, the audience mingled with the performers in a large room behind the stage. Food and drink were laid out on trestle tables; Kate was surprised to discover she was starving, as if she had run a marathon or swum the Channel, instead of just listening to music.

'Did you enjoy it?' Uncle Nicholas asked her,

offering her another sausage roll, and beaming proudly behind his spectacles.

Kate nodded, her mouth full. 'Yes,' she said through the crumbs. 'Gus is dead good, isn't he?'

'He certainly is.' Kate turned; it was the fair-haired music teacher. 'Hello, Nick – how nice to see you all!'

'Hello, Charles. Kate, this is Mr Drummond, Gus's teacher.'

'Pleased to meet you, Kate. Do you like Liszt?'

'Um,' Kate said. But Uncle Nicholas and Mr Drummond started talking about incomprehensible things, and she turned back to the trestle table for some more sandwiches.

Gus had come into the room, and was standing by the door talking to Ned and Charley. Petula was nowhere to be seen. He didn't look pale and exhausted any more; he just looked normal. It was hard to believe he had been creating that wonderful music just a short time ago.

He smiled when he saw Kate, and went over to the table.

'Sandwiches!' he said. 'What an ace idea; I'm starving.'

It was strange to see him with his mouth crammed full of egg sandwich; playing the Liszt, he had seemed almost god-like to Kate. *Surely gods don't eat egg sandwiches*. Kate felt she had to say something to her cousin, tell him how much she had enjoyed his playing.

'I liked your piece,' she said. 'It was good.' It seemed such a feeble thing to say she could have kicked herself, but she felt suddenly shy and tongue-tied.

But Gus seemed to understand. 'Did you?' he said. He looked into her eyes, and smiled again; it was an allies' smile, one friend to another. It was as if he was aware of how the music had affected her. Kate felt a rush of something, a warm feeling for Gus. She smiled back at him, a real smile, one which lit up her whole face.

'It was brilliant,' she said, wonderingly. 'I wish I could play the piano like that.'

Dear Granny,

We all went to a concert at Gus's school last night. Have you heard Gus play? He's just amazing. I think he ought to be on TV, or on the radio or something. He played a Sonarta by List on the Piano. It made me feel really weird, like the music was in my head, or like I wasn't really there. I don't think I can explain it. I just wish I could play music. I used to do Ballet, but I wasn't very good. I'm too fat for Ballet; all the other girls used to laugh at my legs wobbling around. Perhaps I could do Piano instead. I could pay for the lessons.

I still haven't heard from you. Kate thought this sounded too accusing, and added: *Maybe you have written but your letter got Lost in the Post? Please write soon. I would really like to come and live with you.*

With best wishes,

KATE

10
Big Black Lies

They went up to Wales as soon as school broke up for Easter, driving through the evening and into the night. It was late when they arrived; Kate had fallen asleep, and had a vague memory of half-waking to find the car stopped and a dim light on inside, and Aunt Rachel and Uncle Nicholas poring over a map.

She woke again as the car bumped and climbed its way up and along what felt like a cart track. It was very dark outside; tree branches scraped eerily across the windows, as if they wanted to get inside. Kate wondered where on earth they were going. It felt like the Back of Beyond. She had read a poem about the Back of Beyond at school, and now she thought she had arrived there.

At last, they *had* arrived. Uncle Nicholas swung the car through a pair of wooden gates hanging drunkenly off their hinges, and up a pitted driveway. He switched the engine off, and let out a sigh.

'At last,' Aunt Rachel whispered. 'Shall we wake them all up and get inside? I'm dying for a cup of tea.'

'I'm dying for something stronger,' Uncle Nicholas muttered.

'I'm not asleep,' Harry declared loudly, although he had been until a moment ago, his head drooping heavily on Kate's shoulder.

They all stumbled from the car, yawning and rubbing their eyes. Aunt Rachel unstrapped Edward from his car seat and held him tenderly against her; he didn't stir. It was as black as pitch. There were no street lights to illuminate the darkness. There were no lights at all.

'How're you going to find the keyhole?' Gus asked his father.

'My most immediate problem is finding the door. Come to think of it, I'd settle for locating the house,' Uncle Nicholas answered.

In the end he had to switch the car headlights back on while Gus opened the door and let them all in. It smelt musty inside. Aunt Rachel turned on the light switch. Nothing happened.

'Oh, glory,' she said cheerfully. 'I suppose that means the meter is empty.'

'It's probably a power cut,' Ned said gloomily. 'No light, no heat, no hot water, no cups of tea. No –'

'That's right, look on the bright side of things,' Aunt Rachel interrupted him breezily. 'Harry, look in my handbag there for the bag of 50p's. Gus, go and ask Dad for the torch from the car, and then take Charley with you to look for the meter. I think the instructions said it's under the stairs.'

Kate stood with her aunt in the cold, dark kitchen, and wished for the first time in her life that she was at Appleford House. At least there were signs of life there, not like this damp, chilly, unwelcoming place in the middle of nowhere. Even when the meter had been located and fed with money, the car unpacked, cups of tea made and administered, hot baths taken, and beds made up and occupied, Kate still wished she wasn't there. She lay shivering between the icy sheets and listened to the by now familiar sound of Charley snoring. An owl hooted somewhere very close, making her jump. *What an awful place*, she thought grumpily to herself. *Why on earth did they want to come here? I shall never get to sleep. It's far too cold and spooky.*

Things looked considerably better in the morning. Kate was woken from a deep and peaceful sleep by the sun streaming cheerfully through the window and the sound of birds singing happily in the trees. She stretched luxuriously, and felt a curious moment of utter contentment. She couldn't imagine why. Then she swung her legs out of bed – shivering as her bare feet touched the uncarpeted wooden floorboards – and went to explore the cottage.

Everyone else was still asleep. It was very quiet. Kate tiptoed downstairs and into the kitchen; the two younger dogs gave her a hero's welcome and even the old one, Jessie, thumped her tail and grinned at her. Kate had never been alone with the dogs before. She fondled their ears and scratched their cheeks, as she had seen the others do, and was rewarded by their wet noses pushed into the palm of her hand and the feel of their warm, solid, loyal bodies pressing against her legs. *I suppose they're not so bad, really. They're quite friendly. I could get used to having them around. And they* don't *smell, not really; I don't know why I thought dogs always did.*

She found a glass in a cupboard and poured herself some apple juice from the tiny fridge. Then she wandered into the only other downstairs room, which was a dining room and sitting room combined. It, too, had polished wooden floorboards, strewn with rugs; sheepskin ones and pretty pastel patterned ones with a velvety sheen that Kate knew were Chinese, and fringed woollen ones that looked like tapestry. The cushions on the long, low sofa were covered in the same sort of stuff. There was an oak dresser – *a real Welsh dresser!* Kate smiled – with blue-and-white patterned plates and cups and bowls carefully set upon its shelves. The whole room was full of furniture Kate suspected was antique; her parents' house in London had been stuffed with the same kind of thing, but whereas that had been polished and loved and protected, this furniture was scuffed and dusty and ever so slightly scruffy-looking. But the overall effect of the room wasn't scruffy; it looked comfortable and homely and lived-in.

There was an oak chest under the window, and Kate lifted the lid to see what was inside. When she did see, she was enchanted. There was a dolls' house in the chest, but not just any old dolls' house: it was a perfect replica, in miniature, of the cottage. There was the kitchen, and the big downstairs room, and there were the three bedrooms and the bathroom upstairs! It had carrying handles on the roof, and Kate lifted it out of its home in the chest and set it down on the floor. She opened the front, which was hinged all down one side like a door, and looked inside. To her delight, not only was it full of scaled-down furniture, but the furniture matched the cottage's own contents; there was the big round kitchen table, and sofa and chairs, and even the Welsh dresser with the blue-and-white china – only it wasn't china, but paper painted and stuck on.

Kate stood up, and pulled back the heavy gold brocade curtains to let more light in so that she could see the dolls' house better. Then she had her second surprise of the morning. The view from the window was stunning. The cottage was high up – Kate remembered the car climbing up the endless track the previous night – and an unkempt daisy-strewn lawn spread away in front of her before seeming to drop down into the sparkling blue water beyond. On the other side of the water were wooded hills, and beyond them towered mountains, majestic and craggy, their treeless tops dappled by the sun as it moved in and out of the clouds. At the water's edge, far away and below, Kate could just see small fishing boats moored in the harbour, and – to complete her joy – what looked like a fairytale castle, with massive towers at each corner.

Just then, the door opened and Aunt Rachel came in. She was surprised to see her niece standing there.

'Oh!' she said, startled. 'Are you all right, Kate?'

Kate swung round, her face aglow with happiness. 'Oh, Aunt Rachel!' she began. 'I've just found this dolls' house, it's this cottage, look, and it's got all the proper furniture and everything, isn't it clever, and then I opened the curtains and saw outside, and the sea's just down there and look at the mountains, aren't they big, and there's a castle too, and oh, isn't it just *beautiful*?'

Aunt Rachel looked at her niece. She was still in her nightdress; it was too small for her really, the hem too short and exposing her bony ankles and large feet. Her hair was tousled from sleep and she was standing without a dressing gown beside the window, through which Aunt Rachel could feel a draught blowing even from where she stood. But Kate's eyes were shining with a joy her aunt had never before seen there; she looked animated and radiant with pleasure.

Aunt Rachel smiled, and went to join Kate at the window.

'Isn't it?' she said. 'Nicky said there were supposed to be stunning views, but that really is gorgeous.'

Kate pointed towards the castle. 'What's that?'

'I suppose it must be Conwy. And the mountains are Snowdonia.'

Kate shivered suddenly, and her aunt put an arm round her shoulders and drew her close. 'Cold?' Kate nodded, and Aunt Rachel undid her dressing gown and tucked Kate inside with her. 'I'm not surprised, lovey. There's a howling gale coming through that window.'

Kate stood there stiffly for a moment, uncomfortable at the unfamiliar contact. Then all at once she relaxed. Aunt Rachel felt an arm sneak round her waist, and they stood like that in companionable silence, enjoying the sight of the mountains and the sea, until Kate's teeth started chattering and Aunt Rachel sent her upstairs to put something warm on.

*

Kate had never before enjoyed herself as much as she did on that holiday. The sun shone almost every day, and they were out so much they hardly spent any time in the cottage. They went to Anglesey and discovered safe sandy deserted beaches; it was too cold to swim, but they paddled and fished in rock pools and made elaborate sandcastles, and chased the dogs and each other along the edge of the surf with shrieks of joy. They explored Conwy castle, and then drove down to Caernarfon and saw the castle there. They took the steam train to the summit of Snowdon and then walked back down, picnicking at the bottom by a lake whose dimpled grey surface looked like polished pewter.

The last day of the holiday was Kate's birthday. It was grey and blustery, with lowering clouds that threatened rain. Despite the weather, they all voted to spend their last day on the beach. After Kate had opened her presents – even Ned gave her one, a necklace made of shells; he accepted her thanks with a gruff ' 'S OK' – Aunt Rachel packed flasks of hot soup in the picnic basket. They played several games of Dariuses to keep warm, and Kate fell over Max, the brown-and-white dog, landing on the sand with a thump. Uncle Nicholas thought she had hurt herself and ran over to pick her up, but when he reached her he found her doubled up with laughter, and not with pain as he had thought.

'It was so funny,' she gasped, tears of mirth trickling down her face. 'I thought I was flying!'

Uncle Nicholas laughed too, and helped her to her feet. 'Just so long as nothing's broken,' he told her, and kissed the top of her head.

Afterwards Kate and Harry walked along the beach looking for shells.

'Look!' Harry shouted, rushing up to Kate with something in his hand. 'Look, Kate! It's all pearly!' It was a fluted white shell with a mother-of-pearl inside. Kate looked at it, and coveted it.

'Oh,' she breathed, 'isn't it pretty.'

Without any hesitation, Harry pushed the shell into Kate's pocket. 'You can have it if you like, as it's your birthday.' He beamed at her. Then he rushed off again, with Jessie barking joyously at his heels.

On the way home, they all sang 'Happy Birthday' to Kate and 'One Man Went to Mow' at the tops of their voices. Uncle Nicholas suddenly stopped the car outside a pub with light spilling from every window and bright flowers in wooden tubs and window boxes.

'Let's have supper here tonight,' he said, turning to Aunt Rachel. 'You don't want to cook on our last night.'

'We can't!' Aunt Rachel laughed. 'Look at the state of us!' They all looked at each other; their hair was windswept and drizzle-frizzy, and they were all sandy from the beach.

But Uncle Nicholas wouldn't take no for an answer. 'We'll be all right if we just comb our hair and brush the sand off,' he said. 'It's only a pub, not the Savoy!'

So they went in. A delicious smell of cooking greeted them, and there were low beams, and a log fire crackling in the grate. Uncle Nicholas got them all drinks; Kate tasted beer for the first time, a sip from her uncle's glass, and didn't like it very much. They all laughed at her wrinkled nose, and she surprised herself by not minding, and joining in with the laughter. They ate home-made mushroom soup and great chunks of granary bread spread thick with butter, and afterwards a casserole of Welsh lamb with buttery parsley-flecked new potatoes and baby carrots.

'Sebben men wenna mow,' Edward sighed, and fell asleep, his forkful of carrot halfway to his mouth. Aunt Rachel laid him gently down on the settle beside her, and they carried on eating.

Kate was full and could eat no more, but Uncle Nicholas and Gus and Ned all had huge portions of fudge cake. As she sat there, glowing from the wind and warm from the fire, her tummy full of wonderful food, she listened to them all talking about other holidays and agreeing this had been the best ever, and she thought she had never had such a lovely birthday, or been so happy.

When she went back to St Mary's after the holidays, Tamzin noticed the bruise on Kate's leg from where she had fallen over on the beach.

'Has your uncle been hitting you again?' she asked, her eyes wide.

Kate shushed her, and looked around in dismay, but it was too late. Charley had heard.

'What do you mean?' she asked. 'Kate, what does Tamzin mean? You did that in Wales. Dad doesn't hit you! Tell her, Kate!' Her voice rose to an imploring squeak, but Kate didn't say a word. Charley went pink about the ears, and rushed out of the room.

When they were walking home Kate wanted to explain to Charley that it had all been a mistake, she hadn't meant to tell Tamzin such a dreadful thing but it had just slipped out. But she didn't know how to tell her, so it seemed best to say nothing. She could tell Charley was still upset; her shoulders looked very huffy, and she wouldn't look at Kate.

Harry noticed, too. 'Why aren't you talking to Katie, Charley? Charley, why aren't you talking to Katie? Why aren't you? Why? Why?' he kept asking. As they walked up the drive, Kate had suddenly had enough.

'For heaven's sake, don't keep on!' she snapped at him. 'I told Tamzin your dad beat me up. There! Will you shut up now?'

Harry did shut up. He looked at Kate with an expression of horror on his face, his mouth wide open. Then he turned, and ran off up the drive as fast as his short legs could carry him.

Charley looked at Kate too. 'Oh, hell,' she said, with such force that Kate was shocked. 'That's torn it. What did you want to tell him for? I'll have to go after him.' And she, too, hurried up the drive.

Kate, on the other hand, didn't hurry at all. She walked as slowly as she could up the gravel pathway, taking mini pigeon-steps, kicking at loose chippings with her head down. Her legs felt leaden, and she would have given anything to put the clock back, for she knew that Harry had gone straight indoors and told his parents what she had said. She wondered what on earth they were going to say to her.

She didn't have to wait long to find out. A reception committee of Aunt Rachel and Uncle Nicholas was waiting for her in the kitchen. She took one look at their faces, hurt and upset and puzzled and cross, all at the same time, and she wanted to run away. But she didn't. She lifted her chin, and looked them in the eye.

'Yes,' she said defiantly. 'I did say that to Tamzin. So what?'

'You told her Uncle Nicholas hits you?'

Kate nodded once, hard.

'But why? Why did you say that, Kate? Why did you make up such a *wicked* lie?' Aunt Rachel sounded as if she was about to burst into tears. Kate felt like crying, too, but she bit her lip, and the tears at the back of her eyes melted away. She didn't answer; she just stood there.

'Rachel,' Uncle Nicholas said softly, and shook his head. He turned to Kate. 'Can't you tell us? Is someone else hitting you, someone at school, maybe? And you said it was me to cover up for them?'

Kate shook her head vigorously. 'No! Nobody's hitting me. I just said it, all right? I don't know why, I just said it!'

Aunt Rachel stood up, and went over to her. 'Oh, Kate,' she sighed, putting an arm round her. 'Can't you see how silly it was, lovey? If people think Uncle Nicholas has been hitting you, what are they going to think of him, with him being in charge of all these boys?'

That had never occurred to Kate. She felt a great wave of guilt sweep over her, and then resentment in its wake. She shook off her aunt's arm.

'I'm sorry!' she yelled, sounding anything but. 'I didn't mean it. Nobody with any sense would have believed —'

At that moment the kitchen door burst open, and Harry rushed in, red in the face, followed by Charley.

'I hate you!' he shouted at Kate. 'I hate you! My daddy doesn't hit people! He doesn't –'

Charley caught his arm. 'Shut up, Harry,' she told him. 'Just shut up. I'm sorry, Mum; I told him not to come in here, but he just did.'

Aunt Rachel took Harry and Charley out of the room. Uncle Nicholas sat down; he took Kate's hands and drew her to him.

'Kate,' he said gravely. 'Are you still miserable here?' Kate scowled, and shrugged. 'We thought you were beginning to settle down. Listen to me, my dear; if there's any way we can make you feel happier, or more at home, you must tell us. Because, whichever way you look at it, you're stuck with us. This is your home now.'

Afterwards, Kate pondered his words. *Just because we had a good time in Wales, they think I'm happy; they think I'm just going to forget all about Mummy and Daddy, and what's happened, and settle down here. Well, I'm not going to! I'll never be happy here; never ever ever!*

Kate had still had no reply from Granny Greenwood. When they were on holiday, she had decided that if no reply was waiting for her back at Appleford House, she wouldn't write any more letters. The truth was, she *had* felt happy, and more settled; now this had to happen. So she decided to write to her grandmother one last time.

Dear Granny,
*   Why haven't you written? Is it because you don't want me to come? I've done something so awful they're not*

going to want me to stay here any more, even though they pretend they do, so I have to come. I can't stay here; Harry won't speak to me, Charley is being very odd, and I can't bear having to admit to Tamzin that I was lying all the time.

I am going to run away. I have found out the times of the trains. There is one to London from Exeter at 6.30 each morning, so I will try to get a lift to Exeter to catch that one, and then one from London to Reading. I am going to come this Friday. Please don't try to stop me. When I tell you what I've done you'll understand why I can't stay here any more. I hope you don't think I'm an Awful Person when you find out.

With best wishes,

KATE

11

The Great Escape

Kate made her plans very carefully. She was determined that nothing should go wrong to spoil her last, her absolute and final, effort to get away from Appleford House. *This place*, she began calling it to herself. *This Awful Place. Granny will have to take me in if I turn up on her doorstep. She'll simply have to. Won't she?*

By the Thursday, her plans were almost complete. No letter had arrived from Granny, forbidding her to come; no worried telephone call informing Aunt Rachel and Uncle Nicholas that Kate was going to run away. Kate realized the way was clear for her. She looked up the railway timetable again – she had found it in the school library – and discovered that the train she was intending to catch from Exeter actually stopped at Reading, so she didn't need to worry about finding another train from London. Not that London held many terrors for her, having lived there all her life, but it still made things a bit easier. *I could be at Granny's tomorrow in time for elevenses!*

She had packed a bag, the one she used when her class went on the school minibus to the swimming pool in Exeter, and hidden it at the bottom of the blanket box in her bedroom. She had taken most of the blankets out and put them under her bed. They would come in useful the next morning. She would roll them up and put them under the covers when she got out of bed, so that if Charley woke early she would think the hump was Kate, and not notice she was missing.

In her bag, Kate had put a change of clothes and shoes. She would have liked to pack more clothes — she felt sure Granny would appreciate the quality of them, even if Charley and the others appeared not to — but she knew she wouldn't be able to carry her bag if it was too heavy. She put in two photographs; one of her parents, which she had by her bedside in a silver frame, and one taken in Wales on her birthday. Uncle Nicholas had set the timer on his camera to take it, and they were all in the picture, even the dogs. Kate was crouching down at the front of the group, with one arm round Jessie, the old dog, and the other round Edward; she was laughing, her head tipped back slightly, and she looked very happy. She wasn't quite sure why she wanted to take that photograph with her — it wasn't as if she wanted any reminders of Appleford House. *It's because I look happy*, she told herself.

She also put in Spot, the old battered stuffed dog she had had since her first birthday, and some (a very few) school books, including the one with her 'Black and White' poem that Mr Penrose had liked. As an after-thought, she also shoved in the programme from Gus's concert, when he had played the Liszt sonata. Then she rolled up two packets of biscuits, a slab of chocolate and two bananas in a towel and pushed that down the side of the bag. She would have to get up at five o'clock the next morning to be sure to catch the train; it would be far too early for breakfast, and she knew she would have to walk the four miles to Exeter if she couldn't get a lift. On second thoughts, she wasn't sure she still liked the idea of trying to get a lift; it seemed a very dangerous thing to do. That is, supposing there *were* any lifts around at that time of the morning. She had had a vague romantic notion of hitching a ride from a milk float, but it would be a good deal quicker to walk, Kate thought. Besides, the milkman knew Aunt Rachel very well; he would be straight down the drive to sneak on Kate.

''Ere, do you knaw that there niece o' yourn be runnin' away?' Kate could just hear him.

On the top of her bag, Kate packed a spare nightie, her purse containing thirty pounds (all her savings, which she had withdrawn during the week), and her empty sponge bag, which she would put her washing things into in the morning.

All through school on Thursday, Kate was filled with a strange mixture of excitement and dread. She understood the excitement, but not the dread. Her plans were made. They were faultless. Nothing could possibly go wrong. Just to make sure, though, she didn't speak to anybody at school – except Mr Penrose, when he asked her questions – in case anything slipped out.

Tamzin thought this very odd. She at once assumed that Uncle Nicholas had been hitting Kate again; nobody had told her the truth about that, least of all Kate. She badgered Kate all morning, until at last in desperation Kate told her

134

to mind her own business. Tamzin, hurt, did just that.

Then Peggy started. 'What's wrong, Kate?' she asked, in her annoying voice. 'What's the matter? Why are you bein' so quiet?' It sounded like 'quoi-et.'

All at once, Kate had had enough. She turned on Peggy. 'Why don't you just shut up?' she yelled furiously. 'Why don't you just leave me alone? Fat Piggy!'

Peggy's mouth dropped open in dismay, and she turned bright pink. But she didn't say another word to Kate all day.

Back at Appleford House, nobody seemed to notice much that Kate was being exceptionally quiet. Ned was regaling them all with how he had got twenty out of twenty in a maths test; 'the Burner nearly dropped down dead with amazement!' he said. 'Mind you, so did I.' The Burner was the headmaster, Mr Bunson. Kate knew that all the boys called him that.

Then Harry told them his important news. 'Miss Maltby's going to get married,' he said in a small sad voice. 'She told us today. She showed us her enragement ring.'

'That's wonderful!' Aunt Rachel exclaimed. 'I'm so pleased for her. She's been going around with that chap for ages. I wondered if he'd ever get around to asking her.'

'He's called Normal Christmas,' Harry said gloomily. 'She's going to be Mrs Christmas. It's a silly name.'

Kate had to agree. What kind of a name was Normal? But Ned scoffed.

135

'His name's not Normal, it's Norman,' he told his brother.

'It's still a silly name,' Charley declared. 'I could never marry a man called Norman. Or even get married at all,' she added.

'Nobody would ever ask you,' Ned replied, quick as a flash.

They started thumping each other across the table, and the milk jug went flying. Nobody else took the slightest bit of notice.

They all make enough racket to make up for me, anyway. To make up for me, and about five others. Kate thought how peaceful it was going to be living with Granny Greenwood. *Really quiet. Just her and me. Nobody to spoil the peace and quiet; nobody to make a noise. Nobody to talk about how school went, like Charley. Nobody to make silly comments, like Harry. Nobody to bath at night and read stories to, like Edward.* . . . A pang shot through her. She hadn't realized how much she was going to miss Edward. She pushed the thought to the back of her mind. *Don't be so wet,* she said firmly to herself. *Granny will be there. She will talk to me about school (what school?). She will laugh at* my *jokes. She will probably even tell* me *bedtime stories, if I ask her to!*

Even so, Kate felt suddenly depressed. But she wouldn't allow herself to question whether she was doing the right thing. She knew she was, in her heart of hearts.

She picked disinterestedly at her supper until Aunt Rachel noticed.

'What's the matter, lovey?' she asked Kate. 'Don't you feel well?'

'I'm fine; just a bit tired,' Kate told her. That was true, anyway; all the constant going over of plans and memorizing of train timetables had exhausted her. And then there was the horribly early morning the next day to cope with.

But Aunt Rachel provided a way out. 'Why don't you go to bed?' she asked, removing Kate's plate and laying an anxious hand on her forehead. 'Are you sure you're all right? You feel a bit warm.'

Kate assured her aunt she felt fine, and that an early night was all she needed. She got into bed with relief, after first checking that her bag and its contents were still untouched at the bottom of the blanket box, and fell immediately into a deep and dreamless sleep.

Aunt Rachel and Uncle Nicholas were sitting in the kitchen, drinking cocoa. Everyone had finally gone to bed, and they were just about to do the same thing, when somebody rang the door bell.

They looked at each other. 'Who on earth's that, at this time of night?' Aunt Rachel exclaimed. It was almost midnight. 'I hope nothing dreadful's happened.'

Uncle Nicholas opened the door. It was the headmaster, Mr Bunson. He was wearing a dinner jacket and a bow tie.

'Hello, Nicholas.' He smiled apologetically. 'I'm so sorry to bother you at such a late hour, but I was just passing – on my way back from the Old Boys' Reunion – and I saw the light through the door.'

Aunt Rachel stepped forward out of the shadows of the hallway, a worried look on her face. 'There's nothing wrong, is there?'

Mr Bunson shook his head hurriedly and made smoothing motions with his hands. 'No, no, nothing wrong at all. I'm sorry, it was thoughtless of me. I should have waited until the morning. It's just that I meant to pass them on to you earlier, but didn't seem to get the chance, and then I had to go to this dinner, and I didn't realize how late it was until I'd already rung your bell.'

'Pass what on?' Uncle Nicholas asked, curious. 'What's the problem?'

'Oh, there's no problem. The thing is, we had a chap from the Post Office call in today to dismantle the old pillar box – you know, the one at the end of the drive.'

Aunt Rachel nodded. 'Oh, yes, I saw someone heaving away at it this afternoon when I was driving back from the village. I was just thinking what an old one it is – Victorian, isn't it?'

'You're quite right.' Mr Bunson smiled. 'The Post Office have decided they'd like it back, as it isn't operational any more – there hasn't been a collection from it for years. Apparently it's a bit of a rarity, and they want to display it in some kind of museum in Plymouth. I'm not sure of the ins and outs, but the point is they sent someone along today to take it away.' Mr Bunson put a hand in his pocket and pulled out a sheaf of envelopes. 'The Post Office chappy found these in it. He was going to throw them out, thinking it was one of the lads from the school playing games, but then he noticed your name on them.' He peered at one of the envelopes. 'Only it's to some address in Reading. Anyway, he passed them on to me, and I said I'd make sure you got them.' He duly handed them over to Uncle Nicholas, who looked at them curiously.

'Good grief, that's my mother's address!' he exclaimed.

Mr Bunson smiled again. 'I expect it's one of your brood, writing letters to Grandma. Well, mission accomplished; I must be off. Sorry to have bothered you. Goodnight, Rachel!' he called.

'Thanks for taking the trouble, Robert,' Aunt Rachel replied, closing the front door.

Aunt Rachel and Uncle Nicholas looked at each other. 'What on earth . . .' he began. 'Who's been playing games? None of our lot would have posted letters in that box; they all know it's not collected from.'

'One of them doesn't,' Aunt Rachel said slowly. 'I think we'd better open them, Nicky. I think we'll find it's not a game at all.'

When they had read all Kate's letters, Uncle Nicholas gave a huge sigh. 'Poor little devil,' he said, shaking his head. 'I never realized she was still so unhappy.'

Aunt Rachel bit at her underlip. 'She's never really settled down, Nicky. Not really. It must be my fault. How is it I can settle down scores of boys in the house, but fail my own niece? She must have been so miserable . . .'

'Stop blaming yourself!' Uncle Nicholas sounded quite stern. 'It's not your fault. You mustn't think that. When you think what she's been through, the changes that have happened in her life, she's not just going to accept all that without an upheaval, is she?'

'But to want to run away.' Aunt Rachel looked sad. 'Are we so awful? I really thought she was beginning to feel a little happier, after that holiday.'

'But she didn't run away, did she? She's still here, at any rate.' Uncle Nicholas looked more intently at Kate's last letter. 'Hang on a minute – it's dated the twenty-sixth. That's last Monday. And she tells Mother she's coming on Friday. That's tomorrow!'

'Oh, glory!' Aunt Rachel clapped a hand to her mouth. 'We have to stop her. We have to tell her why she can't go and live with her granny.'

When Kate's alarm went off, under the pillow as was now usual, she woke instantly. She didn't feel a bit tired, as she'd expected, just very clear-headed and quite determined. She crept into the bathroom and scraped an almost dry flannel round her face and hands, and brushed her teeth very quietly, under the barest trickle of water. Then she pulled on her jeans and a jersey – it was a chilly morning, although it was almost May – and crept back into the bedroom. She opened the blanket box and extracted her bag; there was a nasty moment when the lid squeaked, and Charley stirred. Kate held her breath in panic, ready to dive into the box and shut the lid if needs be, but it was all right – Charley smacked her lips, and went back to sleep again.

Kate shoved her toilet things into the sponge bag, and pushed it into the big bag, zipping it up with some difficulty as it was full to bursting point. Then she pulled the blankets out from under her bed and arranged them under the duvet in an approximation of a sleeping person. Even for an approximation, it wasn't very convincing; *I wouldn't be fooled*, Kate thought. *Anyone can see it's not a real person – unless it's a very long thin one with no head. How come this sort of thing always works in books? Let's hope Charley doesn't wake up, that's all.* Then she carefully lifted her duffel coat from the hook behind the door, and tiptoed from the room.

When she passed Edward's room she had a sudden urgent desire to go in and kiss him goodbye. She could just picture him lying there, innocent and rosy with sleep, and to her surprise sudden tears sprang to her eyes. *Don't be so idiotic*, she told herself fiercely, wiping her eyes with the back of her hand. *You're not going to miss anything about This Place.* But she knew she would, and it wouldn't just be Edward she missed either.

Going down the stairs, she stepped carefully over the ones she knew creaked. At the bottom she put her jacket on and slung her bag in a more comfortable position over her shoulder. Then she took a deep breath, and opened the front door.

At least, she turned the handle; only she never got as far as opening it, because a hand suddenly came from nowhere and landed on her shoulder. Kate's heart nearly stopped beating, with fright. She whirled around, white-faced. There stood Uncle Nicholas in his dressing gown, and behind him was Aunt Rachel.

'I don't think that's a good idea, Kate,' he said. 'Come on into the kitchen, and we'll talk about it.'

Kate felt like bursting into tears in earnest. All her plans, her careful arrangements, all ruined! *They must have heard me in the bathroom or something, and come to investigate. It's not fair, it's just not fair! Well, they can't stop me – just let them try!*

She took a step backwards, shaking her head

141

fiercely. 'No,' she said loudly. 'I'm not going to talk. I'm going. And you can't stop me!'

Aunt Rachel stepped forwards, holding out her hands. 'Kate,' she said imploringly. 'You can't run away. You simply can't.'

'Yes I can!' Kate shouted. 'You can't make me stay — you can't make me do anything I don't want to do! I'm going to Granny Greenwood's. I've written to her, and she's expecting me, so there!'

Uncle Nicholas gave a deep sigh, and put a firm arm around Kate's shoulders, which she couldn't shake off. 'Kate, you don't understand,' he told her. 'You can't run away because there's nowhere for you to go. Granny Greenwood doesn't live in Reading any more. She doesn't live anywhere. She's dead. She died ten years ago.'

12
Backspeak

Kate felt as if someone had punched her in the stomach.

'Dead?' she whispered, her hand falling from the door handle. Then she shook herself, and tried to wriggle free of Uncle Nicholas's grasp. 'You're making it up!' she accused him. 'She's not dead – she can't be! You're just trying to stop me from going there!'

Uncle Nicholas increased his grip on Kate's shoulders. 'I'm not, Kate. I'm telling you the truth. Your grandmother is dead. I'm terribly sorry.'

Kate made a superhuman effort and threw off her uncle's arm. 'But – but why didn't my mother tell me? She always talked as if Granny was alive. Why didn't she tell me she wasn't?'

'She probably didn't know. None of us knew where your mother was when Granny Greenwood died; we'd completely lost touch. We tried to trace her, to tell her, but we had no luck at all. I'm so sorry, Kate,' he repeated.

Kate suddenly thought of something. 'What about the card?' she asked suspiciously.

'What card?' Uncle Nicholas was mystified.

'The Christmas card – in the cutting-out box.' She clicked her tongue impatiently. 'It had Granny's address in it; "here is my new address", it said. How come you still had that if she died ten years ago?' Kate's voice rose triumphantly; she was sure she'd managed to catch her aunt and uncle out.

But Uncle Nicholas just shook his head sadly. 'There are cards in that box going back years and years. I didn't even know we still had that one. Mother moved to Reading about a year before she died.'

It was slowly beginning to dawn on Kate that she wasn't being tricked, that her uncle was telling the truth. She felt sick.

She looked at Aunt Rachel, who nodded a slow rueful smile. 'It's true,' she said. 'I'm so sorry, Katie darling.'

'Don't call me that!' Kate shouted, furious. 'Just don't call me that!' It was what her father used to call her, 'Katie darling'; it was his special name for her. Nobody else had called her Katie – or darling, for that matter. She didn't want to be called Katie darling again, not ever, and certainly not by this aunt and uncle of hers. It was too painful.

She took her hand from the door knob, determined not to show her feelings of frustration and disappointment and something else she didn't know the name of.

'Anyway,' she said, lifting her chin, 'I wasn't running away. I was just going to stay with her for a while. That's all.'

They led her into the kitchen and made hot drinks, and held her hand and murmured soothing

144

things to her. Kate didn't listen. All she could hear was one voice, going round and round in her head, telling her that there was to be no escaping now. She would have to stay at Appleford House. She had no choice.

Aunt Rachel let her stay at home that day, writing a note for Charley to give Mr Penrose which said that she had been unwell during the night. Kate protested at first, saying she was perfectly all right, but in truth she was glad she didn't have to face everyone at school. She didn't think she could. Even though she had told nobody of her plans to escape to Granny Greenwood's on that Friday, she felt as if everybody knew that she had failed, and that they knew everything she had told them about her grandmother – the infamous, non-existent Mitzi Monroe – had been lies. *As if it's written all through me, in scarlet letters, like a stick of rock: FAILURE, LIAR. And then they'll all laugh at me, and not want to speak to me any more.*

Over the weekend, Aunt Rachel and Uncle Nicholas were particularly nice to Kate. It made her feel very confused. On the one hand, she was still shocked and depressed by the news that Granny Greenwood was dead and wasn't going to be the way out from Appleford House. And on the other hand, she felt oddly comforted by her aunt and uncle's reaction; they hadn't told her off for trying to run away – quite the reverse, in fact. She recalled an occasion when she had tried to run away from home; ages ago it was, she couldn't have been more than about seven. She couldn't even remember what it had been about, just that she had packed a case and heaved it into the kitchen, where her parents were eating lunch. Her father had asked her where she was going. 'I'm running away,' she had said. 'All right then,' he'd replied. 'Don't forget to shut the door behind you, will you?'

But she hadn't gone very far, just sulked behind the rose bushes in the gardens for a bit until her stomach reminded her that she had missed her own lunch. Then she slunk back into the kitchen. Her parents had finished their meal and Kate could hear them talking in the sitting room, but her mother had left her a sandwich and a glass of milk on the kitchen table, with a note. *Glad you decided to come back*, it had said. She made a good deal of noise about eating her sandwich, so they would know she had returned, and afterwards they never mentioned the incident. Kate had been very relieved. She knew she would have felt very silly if they had.

For the first time since arriving in Devon, she started to think about how Aunt Rachel and Uncle Nicholas must feel about her coming to live with them. *First they find out Mummy and Daddy have been killed. Then they discover they have a niece they didn't even know about, and that they've got to look after her – not just for a couple of weeks, but for ever and ever. Then when she gets here she's a right misery guts, and to top the lot she tries to run away.* Kate considered it for a few moments. *But it's been a lot worse for me, hasn't it? At least they've still got everyone and everything they know around them; just me as well, that's all.*

But she knew in her heart of hearts it wasn't that simple and straightforward. She started to feel a sort of grudging sense of pity for them. *I suppose it*

146

can't have been easy having me moping around the place.
Then she heaved a sigh. *Oh, well. It hasn't been easy
for any of us, has it? And it's not going to get any easier.
Not now I know I've got to stay here. Not now I know that
Granny's dead, and there's no alternative. I've just got to
put up with it. But how?*

Going back to school was hard. When she and
Harry and Charley walked into the playground on
Monday morning, a crowd of boys was waiting for
her, led by Miles.

'Who's Mitzi Monroe, then?' he jeered. 'Going
to live in 'ollywood, are yer?'

Kate flushed, and ignored them. But they
persisted.

'You're a liar, Kate Burtons!'

'Liar, liar, pants are on fire!'

Kate pulled Charley into the girls' toilets and
turned angrily to her.

'What did you tell them?' she demanded.

'Nothing!' Charley looked perplexed. 'I haven't
told them anything. Who *is* this Mitzi doo-da,
anyway? They were all talking about her on
Friday.'

'You must have told them. Otherwise how do
they know?'

'Know what?'

Kate scowled. 'About me running away. If you
didn't tell them, Harry must have done.'

But Harry had gone to see Miss Maltby, and
Charley shook her head.

'It wasn't Harry. He doesn't know. Tamzin
wondered why you were away on Friday, and I
said you thought you were going to stay with

147

Granny but you didn't know she was dead, and you were upset. That's what Mum told me; she didn't say you were running away. But Tamzin started going on about America – she thought Granny lived there, for some reason.'

Kate groaned, and put her face in her hands. 'So what did you say?'

'I said she used to live in Reading before she died, but she's never lived in America. I said she must have got her mixed up with someone else.' Charley looked suspiciously at her cousin. 'You didn't tell her Granny lived in America, did you?'

Kate took her hands away from her face and squared her chin. 'Yes,' she said defiantly. 'I did. So what? I didn't know where she lived then. She might have lived in America. She might have lived anywhere. Outer Mongolia – the moon, even.'

To her irritation, Charley laughed. 'Don't be silly! Nobody lives on the moon!'

'I know that.'

'Were you running away? I didn't know. Why were you doing that?'

Kate looked at Charley, who looked back at her, her eyes wide and round and innocent. She really didn't understand why Kate wanted to run away, and what's more she looked at that moment exactly like Peggy, dim and uncomprehending, which irritated Kate even more.

'I was running away,' Kate said, icily deliberate, 'because I couldn't stand it here any more. I hate it here. This rotten school, rotten Appleford House, rotten Devon, and – and your rotten family!' As soon as she said it, Kate knew she shouldn't have. Charley's eyes filled with tears, and her lower lip

148

wobbled. She didn't say anything for a long time, and when she did a fat tear escaped from her lower lashes and slid down her cheek.

'You don't mean that,' she said, her voice trembling. 'I know you don't mean it. Mum said you'd take a long time to get used . . .'

'Oh, socks to your precious Mother!' Kate yelled, exasperated, and flung out leaving Charley to be understanding all by herself.

Things got worse as the day progressed. Miles and Co. hissed 'Liar!' at Kate whenever Mr Penrose's back was turned. Peggy was intrigued by Kate's reasons for making up such stories, and kept on and on.

'Woy did you say 'er name was Mitzi Monroe, Kate? Woy did you say she were an actress? Woy did you say . . . ? Woy, woy, woy?'

Tamzin refused to speak to Kate at all. 'I don't talk to liars,' she announced haughtily. 'All that rubbish about your uncle hitting you, and your famous grandmother,' and she loudly asked Mr Penrose if she could do her project with someone else.

'Certainly not,' he said, but the point wasn't lost on the rest of the class, who all sniggered behind their hands to each other.

'I've told Tamzin not to ignore you,' Charley said at lunchtime. 'I've told her it's not your fault, that you're just unhappy. I've told her –'

'I wish you'd mind your own business,' Kate growled at her, as un-unhappily as she could manage. It was hard to sound convincing, as she felt pretty miserable. It was horrible to be ignored and called names.

149

After lunch, Mr Penrose told the class about secret codes.

'There's lots of codes you can do,' he explained to them. 'For example, one of the easiest is to write down all the letters of the alphabet, in order, and then write the numbers one to twenty-six above the letters. Then you can write messages to each other, using the numbers instead of the letters.' He demonstrated on the blackboard, writing down some of their names. 'There we are. See if you can think up some more codes of your own. Then we'll have a go at cracking them.'

Before too long, someone discovered that writing things backwards was a pretty good code.

' 'Ere,' said Miles, after much thought. 'Did you know my name backwards is Selim Strebor?'

'And mine is Imoan Senoj!' said Naomi Jones, with glee.

Kate spent a few pleasurable moments working out that Mr Penrose's name spelt backwards was Mr Esornep; that Tamzin was Nizmat; that Charley was Yelrahc and Gus was Sug and Ned was Den; and, best of all, the grumpy old school caretaker Fred Flowden was Derf Nedwolf.

Then she was aware of a burst of laughter from Miles's table.

'Sir, Sir!' yelled Miles, spluttering with mirth. 'Kate Burtons backwards is Etak Snotrub!'

The whole class exploded. Kate felt her face flame. *Why didn't I work my own name out? Then I could have thought of something clever to say back.*

'Oh, shut up, Kilometres!' was all she could think of to yell in reply, which even she didn't think was very funny. Neither did anyone else. The entire class was in uproar, laughing at Snotrub, and even Mr Penrose was smiling.

'That's quite enough now,' he said eventually, but it was too late. For the rest of that day Kate had 'Snotrub' whispered at her by the boys. *Oh, well*, she tried to console herself. *At least it's better than 'Liar'*. But she wasn't even sure of that, even though Tamzin smiled sympathetically at her, and whispered 'don't take any notice' once the class had quietened down. Kate went home that evening very fed-up indeed.

Uncle Nicholas was sitting in the kitchen, correcting exercise books, when the three of them walked in.

'Snotrub, Snotrub, Snotrub!' Harry chanted. He had heard Miles and Co. calling after Kate as they left school, and had thought it very funny. 'Daddy, did you know Kate's name backwards is Etak Snotrub?'

Uncle Nicholas glanced up. 'Is it?' he said distractedly. Then he saw Kate's face. 'What's up, my deario?' he asked her.

Kate just shook her head. She felt too full-up to speak, but she didn't know why.

'Harry,' Uncle Nicholas said, 'go and find Mummy. She's talking to Mrs Bunson down by the san. Tell her we need some cakes for tea.' He fished in his pocket and brought out a five-pound note. 'Give her this, Charley. You go too – go and buy yourself some chocolate. Go on now.' He ignored their questions – 'Why, Daddy?' 'We've got plenty of cake, Mum only made some yesterday!' – and ushered them out of the front door.

When he went back into the kitchen, Kate was

sitting at the table. She looked quite exhausted.

'Now then,' he said softly. 'Tell me what's been happening.'

Kate kicked at the table leg. 'I know you only got rid of Charley and Harry to get me by myself,' she said accusingly.

To her surprise, Uncle Nicholas agreed with her. 'Of course I did. You can't tell me what the problem is with their big ears flapping around. Now, are you going to tell me or not?'

Kate was so surprised by his matter-of-fact voice, by his lack of fussing around her, that she found herself telling him all about Tamzin and Mitzi Monroe and Hollywood, and Miles and Liar, the Backspeak code and Snotrub. Uncle Nicholas sat and listened quietly, without interrupting.

'My word,' he said, when she had finished. 'You do have an active imagination, don't you? Mitzi Monroe – what a name!' He chuckled, and then looked serious again. 'Listen, Kate. Children can be very cruel to each other, particularly if there's something different about one of them.'

'There's nothing different about me!' Kate burst out. 'I'm just ordinary.'

'Where *you* come from, yes. But to the local children, you see, you *are* different. You dress differently; you're used to different things. You even talk differently.'

'Not like a local yokel, you mean,' Kate muttered resentfully. It wasn't her who was different. She was perfectly normal. It was the others who were odd.

'And you have rather made things worse for

yourself,' Uncle Nicholas went on. 'Oh, I can understand why you invented a glamorous granny for yourself; Hollywood is so much more impressive than Reading, isn't it? But you must have known they'd find out eventually. In fact, I'm surprised Charley didn't give the whole thing away sooner than she did. No, the problem with making up stories is that you've got to make up even more to cover your tracks.' *Any minute now*, Kate thought, blushing furiously, *any minute now he's going to say something about the lies I told about him hitting me.*

But Uncle Nicholas didn't. Instead, he jumped up from the table and filled the kettle. 'Let's have a cup of tea, shall we?' He plugged it in, and got the cake tin out. 'Oh, good – Charley was right, Rachel did bake yesterday. Have some fruit cake.' He cut two large wedges and set one down in front of her. Then he made the tea, and poured it out into two mugs. 'Now then. The problem as I see it is that you want to fit in at school. At the moment, you feel you haven't any friends.'

Kate stared at him. That wasn't how she saw the problem at all. 'No I don't!'

'I see. Who are your friends, then?'

Kate considered. 'Well – there's Tamzin.'

'I thought you said she was ignoring you?'

'She is, but – well . . .' She floundered around, caught out. 'I don't want to fit in. Not with that lot. I'm quite happy to ignore them, if they want to ignore me.'

'Oh, come on, Kate. Everybody wants to fit in. "No man is an island, entire of itself," and all that.'

Kate looked blankly at him.

'John Donne. Don't suppose you've ever heard

153

of him?' She shook her head. 'Didn't think so. Now listen to me. Instead of ignoring them, why not try doing the opposite? Join in with things – contribute. You see, the trouble with ignoring people is that they might think you consider yourself better than them. We know that isn't true, but if you try and give something back to them, they can see for themselves you're making an effort.'

Kate pulled a face. 'Give something back? What sort of something?'

'Well, let's see. You know what's going on at St Mary's better than I do. There's usually something happening that people are needed for – a sponsored walk, or a fête or something.'

'I don't know.' Kate suddenly thought of something. 'There is a concert next month. Mr Penrose told us about it before half term.'

Uncle Nicholas beamed, and thumped the table triumphantly with his fist. 'There you are then! A concert – perfect! You can perform!'

'Perform what?' Kate scoffed. 'I can't play the piano like Gus, you know. I can't play anything.'

'You don't have to. I expect there'll be enough of that sort of thing.' Uncle Nicholas stood up and cleared the mugs and plates away. 'No. You could do something totally different. Charley told me you used to have dancing lessons. You could do some ballet.'

Kate felt cold with panic. 'No I couldn't! I don't know anything; I haven't had any lessons for ages, and I wasn't any good when I did. I couldn't, Uncle Nicholas. I really couldn't.'

'Yes you could.' Uncle Nicholas looked as if he had made his mind up. 'I could help with the music, and we could get Mrs Bunson to help with the steps – she teaches dancing at a couple of schools in Exeter, you know. And then Rachel could make a costume for you. Have a go, Kate; you can do it!'

Kate protested, but the more she thought about it, the more the idea began to appeal. *I wasn't that bad, actually – that awful snooty Danielle was heaps worse than me, and she thought she was God's gift to dancing. I've still got my shoes, they're in the bottom of my trunk somewhere, and I think I've even got the tunic from when we did that display in Wimbledon. I could do the same dance! I'm sure I could remember it if I heard the music again; perhaps Uncle Nicholas could play it for me. What was it again? Something about the moon, wasn't it?* She got quite excited about it. *Yes, I'll do it! I'll make an effort, like Uncle Nicholas said. I'll show them that I can fit in if I want to.*

13
Shaggy

Kate really warmed to the idea of doing her dance at the school concert. It was having something to work towards, a goal; since she'd gone to live in Devon her only goal had been to get away, but now that was an impossibility it was a relief to have something else to focus her attentions on. *I shall make them all sit up and take notice of me,* she thought defiantly. *I'll show them I'm just as good as they are. I'll show them I don't need any rotten old American granny to make me interesting.* It occurred to her, vaguely, that once the concert was over she would have to concentrate all her efforts on settling down at Appleford House, accepting once and for all that this was now her home. But she didn't want to think about that just yet. She pushed those thoughts to the bottom of her mind and closed the lid on them, like forcing shut an overfilled suitcase.

In the meantime, she had the dance to work out. She found her ballet shoes, a bit squashed but nonetheless still wearable, at the bottom of her trunk, and the tunic from the display too, although it was obvious that she had grown since she last wore it and it would be too small. She showed it to

Aunt Rachel, who held it up against Kate and examined it critically.

'How about if I sew a band of different material round the bottom?' she asked Kate, rummaging around in the bottom of her sewing basket. 'I've got some of this red left over from a summer skirt I made – it looks nice with the white, doesn't it? Or look, here's some pale green. Good heavens, that was what I used for some pyjamas I made Ned. He could only have been about four!' A dreamy look came over Aunt Rachel's face as she remembered the four-year-old Ned – *I hope he was better then than he is now*, Kate thought sourly. *Why can't I have a new tunic? Why do I have to have the old one with a chunk of red stuff stuck on the bottom?*

'What do you think would be best?' Aunt Rachel asked her, still looking lost in the past. 'What's the dance about?'

'The moon,' Kate muttered, swinging her dancing pumps. It sounded silly, somehow, said out loud like that.

'Oh, lovely,' said Aunt Rachel. 'Well, I think the green, then, don't you? I could make a sash too, and sew some round the armholes; that'll look better than just a great lump of it tacked on to the hem. I should have enough fabric. . . .' She held out the material in front of her, measuring it with her eye; she looked very professional, the dreamy look quite gone. 'What about your shoes?' she asked Kate suddenly. 'Do they still fit? I'm not sure we can run to a new pair, and I can hardly make ballet shoes out of leftover material!' She laughed, but a twinge of irritation stirred in Kate. *Why do they have to be so poor? And why do they always have to sound so* cheerful *about it, as if it's something to be proud of?*

Kate shrugged. 'They're OK,' she said grumpily.

Aunt Rachel didn't seem to notice the tone of Kate's voice. 'I do think it's a nice idea,' she told her, ripping the material in half, 'you doing this dance for St Mary's. I had no idea you took ballet lessons in London. We must have a word with Mrs Bunson, and see if she can fit you into one of her classes. Would you like that?'

'Not really,' said Kate, quite rudely. The idea of fat, middle-aged Mrs Bunson teaching her ballet was appalling. 'Why are you ripping that stuff up? Can't you afford scissors?' she added nastily.

But Aunt Rachel thought she was joking, and smiled. 'If you tear it, it goes along the weave and you get a straighter line,' she told Kate. 'I think this is going to look really pretty, don't you?'

Kate doubted it, but realized with a guilty pang that Aunt Rachel was only trying to be helpful; she couldn't help it if they were poor. Uncle Nicholas was helpful too, Kate conceded; suddenly, over supper that evening, she remembered how the song that accompanied the dance went, and she sang a snatch to him.

Uncle Nicholas frowned. 'I'm not sure . . .' he began.

'You must know it,' Kate said, frustrated, and leapt up from the table. The rest of the family looked at her, amused, but she didn't notice. 'Listen,' she told her uncle, and rushed into the sitting room where the piano sat, its black-and-white teeth grinning up at her in an unhelpful way. 'Listen,' she repeated, and struck a note experimentally. To her surprise it sounded right; she struck another, and another, feeling her way around until she had found the bare bones of the music she could hear playing in her mind.

'This is the song – listen,' she told her uncle, and played it again. 'It's about the moon; you must know it, you simply must,' she pleaded.

To her intense surprise, Uncle Nicholas recognized it.

'Good Lord,' he said, looking amazed. 'I do, too. It's *Clair de Lune* – it's by Debussy, from the *Suite Bergamasque*. Who taught you to play it?'

Kate couldn't have cared less if it were Baa Baa Black Sheep from the Three Piece Suite by Mozart; the fact was, Uncle Nicholas knew it.

'Nobody taught me,' she said impatiently. 'I just found it. Can you play it?'

Uncle Nicholas laughed. 'Of course I can; it's pianists' bread and butter.' He sat down at the piano and played it, all of it, the chords in the left hand too, which Kate hadn't attempted to find.

When he had finished, Kate smiled at him. 'That's it,' she said. 'I remember it now – I remember the dance.' She couldn't wait to get started.

Uncle Nicholas recorded the music for her, and lent her a small cassette player to play it on.

'Only you mustn't call it a song,' he told her. 'It's a tune, or just a piece of music. Songs have words.'

'Always?' she asked, surprised. She knew songs had words, but she hadn't known it was wrong to call other things songs.

'Always,' said Uncle Nicholas firmly. She

159

supposed it was being a music teacher that made him so sure.

For the next week, Kate worked hard on her dance. She found herself remembering more and more of the steps, and singing the music to herself at odd times and in odd places, like in the bath and going upstairs. She shut herself away after school every day in the large bathroom, which was as big as a bedroom and had a heated chrome towel rail fixed to the wall, which was useful as a *barre*. She knew she had to do exercises to warm up before she started, and she did them religiously; she could almost hear the gentle wavering voice of Miss Braithwaite as she stood there, hand on the towel rail: 'Bend, two three, and stretch, two three, and *plié*, two three – that's very good Danielle. Kate dear, don't stick your rear out; it makes you look like a duck.'

Rear indeed, Kate thought scornfully, as muscles she'd forgotten she had screamed in protest at the unaccustomed hard work. *Why couldn't the silly old bag say 'bottom', like everybody else? Bottom, bottom, bottom!* It helped her forget how her legs ached, and to concentrate on getting the dance right.

By Saturday, the aching muscles felt better, but Kate wasn't entirely happy that she had remembered all the steps properly. The beginning and the end were all right, she could remember those perfectly; but there was a largish chunk in the middle she just couldn't recall. She tried making a few things up, and in between times stood there and waved her arms around in what she hoped was an artistic manner. *Port de bras*, it was called, what you did with your arms in ballet. Miss Braithwaite had been very keen on a good *port de bras*. Despite Miss Braithwaite's inability to say the word 'bottom', Kate half wished she was there to help with the middle of the dance. *It's still not right*, she said to herself. *It's no good; I'm just going to have to show somebody, and ask them what they think*. She threw a towel round her shoulders to keep herself warm, and went downstairs in search of help.

Aunt Rachel was in the kitchen, making pastry. 'Hello, Kate,' she greeted her. 'You look hot. Have you been dancing?'

'Can you come upstairs a moment and watch me?' Kate began. 'It's just –'

'Oh, lovey, any other time I'd be pleased to,' Aunt Rachel interrupted, raising her floury hands from the mixing bowl. 'Only I'm in the middle of making this pie for the bring-and-buy this afternoon, and I really must get it finished. Give me ten minutes, all right?'

'It's OK,' Kate said with dignity. 'It's not important. I'll find somebody else.'

She went into the sitting room, where Uncle Nicholas and Harry were engrossed in making a model aeroplane from an Airfix kit.

'Uncle Nicholas,' she said. 'Can you come and watch me for a moment? I just want –'

'Be with you in a tick,' Uncle Nicholas said. He sounded miles away. 'Look, Harry, that bit goes in there, can't you see? Watch what you're doing with the glue – I said *watch it*! – oh, good grief, don't tell your mother. She'll go spare!'

Kate realized her dance wasn't going to get a look-in, and went out of the room. In the hallway, Ned and Gus – home for the weekend, as usual –

were sniggering about something Kate guessed was rude, because they stopped with difficulty when they saw her.

'Hello, Kate,' Gus said, clamping his mouth shut to stop a snigger from escaping.

'Hello,' she replied. 'I don't suppose . . . ?' She stopped. *No. Of course they wouldn't want to see it. It's music Gus knows about, not ballet.*

'Don't suppose what?' Ned asked her. He looked at her curiously. She was wearing the royal-blue leotard the girls at St Mary's wore to do PE, and with the towel round her shoulders and her hair scraped off her face and into a rubber band, she supposed she did look rather odd. Even so, what Ned said next was very rude.

'What have you been doing?' he asked pleasantly. 'Keep Fit? Or is it Keep Fat?' He and Gus burst into fresh guffaws, and Kate, her face flaming, pushed past them and up the stairs. *The pigs!* she thought furiously. *The rotten, stinking pigs!*

Charley came out of the bedroom, dressed in a holey T-shirt and a pair of boy's shorts that were much too small for her. She was carrying her bathing costume.

'Hi!' she said, smiling at Kate. 'Have you finished in the bathroom now? I want to get a towel; Becky's just rung up to ask me to go swimming. D'you want to come too?'

Kate sighed. 'No,' she said. 'I've got to finish my dance. Will you watch me a moment?'

'Can't,' Charley called from the bathroom. 'Becky'll be here in a sec. We're going to practise diving from the top board. It's dead good – are you sure you don't want to come?'

But Kate knew Charley was only being polite, because she grabbed a towel and was off down the stairs and out of the front door, yelling goodbye and ignoring her mother's comment of 'you're not going out dressed like that, are you?' She hadn't even waited for Kate's answer.

Oh, well. That's it, then. I'll just have to work it out for myself, as nobody else is interested. Kate went back into the bathroom, but her heart was no longer in the dance. She decided to get changed instead. As she was pulling her sweatshirt over her head she looked up, and there stood Edward in his vest and pants. He had obviously just woken from his afternoon nap. He beamed at Kate, and her heart lifted, just a bit. She always felt better when Edward smiled at her. *At least he wants me.*

'Hello,' she said, going to him and lifting him up. 'Would you like me to read you a story?' And she sat down with him on her lap. But he wouldn't sit still.

'No,' he protested, wriggling. 'Get down!'

Kate felt a sharp stab of disappointment. 'All right,' she snapped. 'Be like that, you little ratbag!'

Edward stopped wriggling abruptly and looked up at Kate, his lower lip quivering at the crossness in her voice. Kate relented.

'What would you like to do, Edward?' she asked him.

'Walk,' he replied. 'Edward Kate go for little walk.'

Suddenly, Kate had an idea. 'Edward,' she said slowly, 'would you like to go and see the ponies?'

'Yesh,' he said positively. 'Go see the ponies!'

*

It had seemed a good idea at the time, but when they got off the bus at Two Bridges, Kate wasn't so sure. It had been a long bus ride, ten miles or more, and at first Edward had been content to sit quietly on Kate's lap and look out of the window, but he soon got fed up with that, and became very restless. They were both glad when the bus let them off. So, Kate suspected, were the other passengers.

'Mind how you go, m'dears,' the driver called to them. 'Don't you go gettin' caught in that there rain, now.' The doors closed with a mechanical swish, and the bus drove off.

It was very quiet when it had disappeared away down the road. The weak, watery sunshine of the morning had gone, and in its place was unrelieved grey sky, with a nasty big black cloud back in the direction they had come from. Kate shivered, and took Edward's hand.

'Come on,' she told him. 'Let's go and look for some ponies. Do you remember the baby one we saw here on your mummy's birthday?'

Edward nodded. 'Shaggy,' he said. 'Baby horsy called Shaggy.'

Kate was surprised he remembered. 'That's right! It was, too.' They left the road and began to walk in a southerly direction across the coarse sheep-cropped grass.

They walked for a long time, hand in hand, over the rough hummocks. Edward sang as they walked, tuneless wordless little hums, and Kate thought. She thought about her dance, and the imminent concert, and about St Mary's itself, and how the children were beginning to talk to her again, the lies she had told forgiven if not forgotten.

Then she thought about Appleford House. She realized with a start that the reason she had been so cross earlier about Aunt Rachel and Uncle Nicholas's apparent lack of interest in her dance was because they usually *did* seem interested in what she was doing. *Look at how they helped me; Aunt Rachel with the costume, and Uncle Nicholas with the music. They are interested in me – if I'm being fair I know they are. It's just that they're so different from Mummy and Daddy. I had to share them with their work, but I knew about that; I was used to it. I knew they ran their business from home, and had to go off on business trips quite often. It's just what happened. But when they were around I had all their time, I had them all to myself. Not like here, at Appleford House. When Aunt Rachel and Uncle Nicholas are around they're really busy, and anyway I always have to share them with the others; the cousins, and the boys in the House. But that doesn't mean they don't care about me. Does it?*

She suddenly remembered the look on Uncle Nicholas's face at Pevensie College the night Gus played the Liszt sonata, and she was filled with a feeling of certainty that her aunt and uncle cared about her. *Of course they do. And they were so proud of Gus that night. I want them to be proud of me, too, when I do my dance.*

'Look!' Edward shouted suddenly, pulling his hand from hers. 'Horsies! Over there!'

Sure enough, there in front of them was a group of Dartmoor ponies, and standing slightly separate from the group was a foal that looked very similar to the one they'd seen on Aunt Rachel's birthday. Edward began to run towards them on his stumpy little legs, windmilling his arms and yelling. 'Shaggy!' he shouted. 'Shaggy!'

'Come back!' Kate called. 'Edward, come back! You'll frighten them! Come back!'

But it was too late. The ponies looked up, startled, and galloped away. When Kate reached Edward he was waving goodbye to them.

'Horsies gone now,' he told Kate. 'Bye-bye horsies.' He seemed quite unconcerned.

Kate sighed. 'That's because you frightened them, twitface.' She took his hand. 'Come on. We'd better be getting back.'

They turned and trudged back the way they had come. The black cloud had got much bigger; it seemed to be covering most of the sky now, and as they reached the edge of it it started to rain, big splashing drops the size of tenpences.

Edward hunched his shoulders and started to complain. 'Edward getting wet,' he moaned. 'Don't like it.'

Kate started to hurry, pulling him along with her. 'Don't make such a fuss,' she told him briskly. 'It's only a drop of rain.' She sounded just like her mother.

They stumbled their way across the uneven hummocky ground for that seemed like an eternity. It was raining with a vengeance now, the rain plastering their hair to their heads and making Kate's skirt stick clammily to her legs. Edward began to cry, howling as Kate dragged him along with gritted teeth, then he just grizzled, and then eventually he was silent.

'It's not far now,' Kate kept saying to him. 'It's not far, I promise. We'll soon get to the bus stop, and then we can go home.' But it was far. Kate began to wonder if they would ever reach the road;

166

she wondered if somehow they were going in totally the wrong direction, away from the road instead of towards it. *I'm sure this is the right way. It has to be, it just has to!* She realized, with a certainty that sat in her stomach like a lead pudding, that they were lost. Lost on Dartmoor, in the pouring rain, with no coats and with her two-year-old cousin to look after. She suddenly remembered that nobody knew where she was, and nobody knew Edward was with her; in her pique, she had just yelled 'I'm going for a walk' as the front door slammed behind them. *Oh, no. What are we going to do? But I mustn't panic; I mustn't show Edward I'm worried. Oh, God. Oh, Aunt Rachel. Oh, Uncle Nicholas. Oh, anybody!*

She kept going across the moor, dragging Edward with her. He was so tired he could barely walk; she made him climb up on to her back, and he wrapped his arms tightly round her neck and promptly went to sleep. He bumped around as she walked, and kept sliding down, so she had to stop every few steps and hitch him back up. He was very heavy, and she was getting extremely hot; the sweat ran down her face and mixed with the rain and slid, stinging, into her eyes. The path through the heather, already churned up by sheep's and ponies' hooves, had been turned by the rain into a sticky muddy morass. Kate's feet, unsuitably clad in summery sandals, were getting so bogged down she could scarcely lift them for each new step. *This is like torture. I can't stand it any longer. Please let me find the road – oh, please!*

And suddenly there it was, a wet black ribbon stretching in front of them from left to right as Kate came to the top of a slight ridge. She slipped and slid her way down to it, Edward bumping around on her back but seemingly quite undisturbed. Of Two Bridges and the bus stop there was no sign. *But at least it's the road; something is bound to come along eventually, isn't it?*

Just at that moment a car came slowly along the road towards them, its headlights penetrating the gloom. As it approached, Kate could see that its windscreen wipers were working overtime. She simply didn't have the energy to wave it down, so stood where she was, in the middle of the road with the rain thrumming down around her, and trusted that it would see her in time. As the car drew to a halt, she had a sudden moment of panic; it had always been drummed into her that she should never, on any account, accept lifts from strangers. Her mother had told her dreadful stories of children who got into strangers' cars and were never seen again. *But this is different. This is An Emergency.*

The head that poked from the car window didn't look like a murderer's. It was a lady, with a neat short hairstyle and pearl earrings.

'What on earth . . . ?' the head said, and then, 'Oh, my goodness me!' The head disappeared inside the window. 'It's a little girl, George,' Kate heard her say. 'A little girl carrying a toddler; they're soaked!'

The driver's door was thrown open, and a man holding a raincoat over his head got out. Kate supposed he was George. He didn't look like a murderer either, she thought, although by then she wouldn't have cared if he'd had horns and a forked tail. He opened the rear door of the car and lifted Edward from Kate's back. Gently ushering her inside, he put the still-sleeping Edward on her lap, and covered them both with a tartan rug. Then he got back into the car and drove off.

The lady kept turning round and looking at them, a concerned expression on her face. She was talking to Kate; Kate could tell because the lady's mouth was opening and shutting, like a goldfish in a bowl, but she couldn't tell what she was saying. *I'm so tired. So tired. Just let me rest for a minute. . . .*

She eventually realized the lady was asking where they lived. With her last bit of strength, Kate managed to mumble Appleford House's address. Then she closed her eyes, with relief, and went to sleep.

14
Clair de Lune

Kate and Edward both woke up as the car stopped on the sweep of drive outside the school. By now the heavy rain had turned into a thin Devon drizzle, and there was a small knot of people clustered together on the drive. Kate recognized Uncle Nicholas and Mr Bunson amongst them, and a horrible sick wormy feeling grew in her stomach. The man driving the car got out first, and went over to talk to Mr Bunson. His wife turned round in the passenger seat.

'Oh, you're awake!' she said to Kate. She smiled; she had a very nice, kindly smile, but it didn't make Kate feel better at all.

'Now don't you fret,' she said. 'They might be a bit angry with you at first, but it'll just be worry, and the relief of having you back safe and sound. Let's get you indoors, shall we? You'll be wanting to get out of those wet things, and your little brother too. My, but I bet your mum'll be glad to see you!'

Kate didn't have the heart or the energy to tell her Edward wasn't her brother, and she didn't have a mum. They got out of the car and followed the lady to the front door, Edward rubbing his eyes and whimpering slightly. The door was suddenly thrown open with a burst, and Aunt Rachel flew out; her hair was all on end, as if she had just got out of bed, and her face looked as if she had been crying.

'Mummy!' said Edward, with a sob, and hurled himself at her.

Kate didn't know what to do. The lady was talking to Aunt Rachel – about worry, and relief, and hot baths – and Aunt Rachel was trying to comfort Edward, and saying 'yes, yes' in a distracted sort of way. Charley and Harry appeared out of the front door and stood, wordlessly, next to their mother, staring at Kate with huge frightened eyes.

'What on earth's the matter?' Kate asked Charley, irritated by her silence. 'We're back now. We're OK. Do stop *staring* at me like that!'

But Charley didn't reply.

The man was talking to Uncle Nicholas. 'Harris is the name,' he was saying. 'Found your little girl on the road up on Dartmoor – just materialized in front of the car. Lucky I saw her in time; dreadful weather for May! I don't think she's hurt – or the little one – just exhausted. The wife and I are on holiday down here; had a devil of a job finding your place.'

He went on and on, and so did his wife, to Aunt Rachel. Kate wished they would all just shut up and let her go inside and put on some warm dry clothes and have something to eat. It was just like being in a nightmare.

At last, they did all shut up. Uncle Nicholas shook the Harrises' hands and thanked them, and they drove off through the drizzle.

171

'Crumbs,' said Kate, as Uncle Nicholas closed the front door. 'Didn't they go on? I thought they'd never shut up and go away.'

Aunt Rachel, halfway up the stairs with Edward in her arms, whirled round. 'You're jolly lucky they came along when they did,' she said, in an icy voice. She snapped her mouth shut into a pinched white line, and would have gone back up the stairs, if Kate hadn't continued.

'They were so boring,' Kate said. 'They just droned on and on, and all I wanted to do was go to sleep.' It wasn't that she wasn't grateful to Mr and Mrs Harris for rescuing her and Edward. It was just that she had been very frightened, and now she was relieved, and the relief made her sound rude.

But Aunt Rachel clearly didn't see it like that. She stormed down the stairs and pushed the protesting Edward into Uncle Nicholas's arms. Then she faced Kate.

'Boring, were they?' she demanded. Her voice was no longer icy and controlled, but shaking with rage. 'You ungrateful child! Do you realize that if it hadn't been for them you'd still be wandering around on Dartmoor? Do you? With *my* son! Going off in a sulk by yourself is one thing – we've come to expect it of you – but taking Edward with you is quite another. Didn't you realize we'd be worried sick?'

Uncle Nicholas told Charley to take Edward upstairs. He took a step towards his wife, but she lifted an arm as if to ward him off.

'But of course you wouldn't care, would you?' she went on. 'You wouldn't care that we've had half the school out looking for you, and the parents

172

from the bring-and-buy, and the police. You wouldn't care that you've wasted all these people's time because of your – your petulance! I wouldn't even put it past you to have done it deliberately, just to teach us some sort of lesson, but what I don't know. What is it with you, Kate? Why do you think you have the monopoly on unhappiness? Why do you have to punish everyone around you for what's happened to you? It's not our fault your parents died!'

Ned, drawn from the sitting room into the hall at the unusual sound of his mother's voice raised in anger, looked shocked at this.

'Steady on, Mum!' he said.

But Aunt Rachel appeared not to hear him. Her eyes were two dark flashing holes in her white face, blazing furiously at Kate. Kate was frightened, but fascinated at the same time, like a rabbit she had once seen, caught in Uncle Nicholas's headlights on the front drive, frozen with fear and quite unable to move off the road to safety.

'You come into our house,' Aunt Rachel raged on, 'and we take you into our family, with love, and what do we get in return? Silence, and sulks, and dreadful lies, and attempts to run away! What did you think you were running away from, Kate? Your problems aren't with us, they're inside you. You can't run away from them, you stupid, ungrateful child – and you can't run away from us. You're stuck with us. And we, God help us all, are stuck with you! D'you hear me?' And she put her hands on Kate's shoulders and shook her. Kate's teeth rattled, and for one horrible, heart-stopping moment she was truly afraid. She thought Aunt Rachel had gone mad.

But Uncle Nicholas laid a hand on her arm. 'That's enough, Rachel,' he said firmly, in the same sort of voice he might use for one of the boys in his house. 'That's enough, now.'

Slightly to Kate's surprise, Aunt Rachel's hands dropped from her shoulders, her body sagged, and the anger and fire went out of her eyes.

'Go upstairs now, Kate,' Uncle Nicholas said crisply. 'Get out of those wet things and have a hot bath. Quickly now. I'll be up shortly.'

Kate did as she was told. She could hardly get up the stairs fast enough. She felt numb, confused and muddled; things were happening that shouldn't be, the order of things was upset. Aunt Rachel losing her temper – *she looked mad*, Kate thought, shuddering, *she looked as if she wanted to kill me* – and Uncle Nicholas unexpectedly, unusually, taking charge.

She walked unsteadily into the bathroom to find Charley in there, drying Edward after his bath. Edward, pink and rosy and revived by the hot water, and oblivious of the drama that had taken place downstairs, turned and beamed at Kate.

'Us saw Shaggy,' he said, and turned to his sister. 'Tarley, Kate 'n' Edward saw Shaggy.'

'We did, didn't we,' said Kate, hugely relieved that Edward, at least, appeared to be none the worse for wear. 'It was good fun, wasn't it?'

Charley snapped her head round and glared at her cousin. 'How you've got the nerve!' she exclaimed. 'If you knew how worried Mum and Dad were . . . ! *And* the police came looking for you.

They were just about to get tracker dogs and everything, and then you come swanning up the drive after being missing for hours and hours, and say you had fun!'

This was too much. 'I didn't!' Kate protested. 'I didn't do that! And I didn't know about the police. I was only –'

'Oh, just shut up!' Charley's eyes flashed exactly the way her mother's had done five minutes earlier. 'I'm fed up with you! I've tried to be friends, I've tried to be nice to you, but nothing's worked. I don't see why I should bother any more. You're a mean horrible fat pig, and I hate you!' And with that, Charley rushed from the bathroom, bundling a bewildered towel-clad Edward in front of her.

Kate filled the bath with scalding water and climbed in. Up to her neck in bubbles, she tried to work out why she felt so strange. Then she realized it was because she wasn't feeling anything. *Numb. I feel numb. What's the matter with me? Why don't I feel glad to be back, not wandering around on that horrid moor in that horrid rain any more? Why don't I feel miserable at Aunt Rachel yelling at me like that, or frightened at her shaking me? Why don't I feel ashamed, or upset at what Charley said, or embarrassed at Ned hearing it all, or – or anything? Why didn't I cry when Mummy and Daddy died – why haven't I been able to cry since? What's wrong with me? Why don't I feel?*

In a sort of desperation, Kate pinched the top of her arm between her fingers and thumb, hard, until when she let go the imprint of her fingers remained, angry red marks on the flesh and a bruise beginning to form. *I felt that, all right. That'll give Tamzin something to look at in PE on Monday.* But it wasn't the sort of thing she wanted to be able to feel.

After her bath, she didn't know what to do. She couldn't face going downstairs, so she put her nightie on and got into bed. Presently, Uncle Nicholas came up, his face expressionless. He brought with him a tray with a bowl of soup and a beefburger and some baked beans on a plate.

'Here we are,' he said, setting the tray down on the bedside table. 'It's not cordon bleu, I'm afraid, but it's the best I can do.'

From that, Kate deduced he had cooked it himself. She expected him to go downstairs again, but he didn't. He perched on the side of the bed and watched Kate eat, as if suspecting she would leave it once his back was turned. *Fat chance of that – I'm starving.*

She cleared the plates, and lay down again with a heavy sigh. Uncle Nicholas stacked the dishes on the tray, his features still carefully composed, and went to leave the room. Then he seemed to change his mind. He put the tray down and sat back on the bed.

'Kate,' he said slowly. He rubbed his chin with his hand, thoughtfully; he gave the impression of someone who had been asked a tremendously important question, the one that wins the star prize, the foreign holiday or the car, in a TV quiz show. *If he gets it wrong, he loses the prize*, Kate thought. *But what was the question? I didn't ask him anything.*

At last, Uncle Nicholas spoke again.

'Rachel was upset,' he said. 'She was terribly worried about you both; it's a serious thing, you

176

know, being lost on Dartmoor. Particularly in this weather. She said some things she didn't mean. Don't take it too much to heart.' He gazed at his niece's face, bland and sulky, and wondered what she was thinking. 'And she was wrong, Kate. About us being stuck with each other, I mean. If you truly hate it here – if you dislike us all as much as you appear to – I'm sure an alternative can be found.'

Kate stared at him. What did he mean? *Is he trying to tell me he wants me to go?* She was filled with a sudden panic. *But where would I go to?* She swallowed. 'What – what alternative?' she croaked.

'I don't know. But we could think of something; I'm sure we could. If you loathe it here so much that you have to run away.'

They looked into each other's eyes, Uncle Nicholas's gaze calm and level and Kate's wild and panic-stricken, searching for another meaning behind his words. *But I don't want to go!* she wanted to tell him. *I want to stay here! I wasn't running away, it was all a – misunderstanding. I don't hate you all! I like you, really I do!*

But the words stuck in her throat, and the moment passed. Kate looked away.

'I dunno,' she muttered.

'Well, think about it.' Uncle Nicholas picked up the tray and went to the bedroom door. It was still raining, and gloomy enough for the light to be on even though it was still only half past seven. 'Goodnight, Kate.'

He snapped the light off.

'Uncle Nicholas!' The urgency in Kate's voice nearly made him turn it back on again.

'What's the matter?'

'I – I'm sorry. About today – you know.'

There was a long silence. Uncle Nicholas stood in the doorway, silhouetted against the landing light, the tray balanced on his hip.

'So am I,' he replied at last. Kate couldn't see his face, but his voice sounded sad. Sad, and infinitely tired. 'So am I.'

That Friday, it was the concert at St Mary's, when Kate was to dance her solo. She practised it with little enthusiasm during the week; Mrs Voysey, the teacher organizing the concert, had put it down on the programme, but Kate wasn't sure any more if Aunt Rachel and Uncle Nicholas were going to come. *If they're not coming, I don't want to do it,* she thought. *What's the point? I want them to feel proud of me, like they were of Gus when he played the Liszt sonata. How can they, if they're not even going to be there to watch me?*

She wasn't sure why she didn't think her aunt and uncle were going to attend the concert. To her relief, nothing more had been said about her escapade on Dartmoor and the events that followed, except by Edward when she was bathing him. In fact he mentioned it most nights.

'Us had fun,' he said, conspiratorially. Or, 'Shall we go see Shaggy again, Kate?' Kate was glad that Edward, at any rate, hadn't suffered any ill effects from the episode.

But Aunt Rachel had made no mention of her

outburst, and Uncle Nicholas hadn't spoken again of any 'alternative arrangement'. But, for all that, things weren't back to normal. They had changed. The atmosphere was subtly different. Kate had the feeling her aunt and uncle were biding their time before telling her of the alternative arrangement they had made. There were only two possibilities Kate could think of. *Foster parents – years and years of Mr and Mrs Shaddocks*. She couldn't bear that. But the alternative was even worse. *An Orphanage*. The very word sent a shudder down her spine.

She was looking for her dancing tunic and shoes that evening when Charley burst into the bedroom.

'There you are!' she said. 'Mum says to hurry up, everyone's waiting for you.'

'Everyone?' Kate frowned. 'You mean – you're all coming?'

Charley sighed impatiently. 'Course we are. It's mine and Harry's school concert too, remember? Anyway, we all want to see your dance. You've been making so much fuss about it.'

Kate bit back the reply she wanted to make. 'And Ned's coming too?' she said instead. She didn't like the thought of that, although she was pleased that everyone else would be there in the audience, rooting for her.

'I just said so, didn't I?' Charley sounded even more impatient. She always sounded like that with Kate, these days.

Kate bent down and looked under Charley's bed. 'I'll be down in a moment. I can't find my things. You haven't seen them, have you?'

Aunt Rachel appeared in the doorway, holding a

carrier bag. 'Are you looking for these, Kate?' It was the missing tunic. 'I put them in a bag for you, and Mrs Sadler put them away in the cupboard under the stairs. She must have decided it was a duster or something, although what she thought ballet shoes were doing in a bag with a duster, I cannot imagine. Wretched woman. I told Nicky it would be easier just to carry on doing the house-work myself, but he did insist, and Brenda Bunson has nothing but praise for her. Still, I suppose Brenda hasn't got six children to complicate things. . . . Come on, Kate, do; we're going to be late. We haven't got time to stand around chatting.'

Kate hadn't said a word, and felt Aunt Rachel was being unfair. But she followed her meekly down the stairs. She was too nervous about the concert to protest. And she didn't think her aunt would listen; she just didn't seem to have time for her any more.

Kate had always thought that nerves dis-appeared once you were onstage. Everything she had ever heard or read about performing had told her that. The thought comforted her as she shook when Mrs Voysey put make-up on her face – 'just a little, dear, or the audience won't be able to see your pretty face' – and when her fingers were so cold and numb that she couldn't do her shoes up and she had to ask Tamzin, who was a rat in the fourth form playlet about the Pied Piper of Hamlin, to do them up for her.

Even Tamzin told her the same thing. 'Don't worry – you'll be OK once you get out there,' she assured Kate, her familiar face strange beneath its stuck-on black nose and painted whiskers. 'It's easy-peasy, honestly.'

But Kate didn't feel OK. If anything, she felt worse, as the recording Uncle Nicholas had found for her began to thread out the by now well-known notes of the Debussy, and Kate realized with a kind of chill horror that she couldn't remember a step of the dance. She stood there, frozen to the spot, her heart beating frantically beneath the thin cotton of the tunic, and gazed out into the audience. *If I could only see Aunt Rachel*, she thought. *She might be able to help. She knows what I'm supposed to do.* But she couldn't see anything beyond the spotlights which were shining down on to her face, dazzling her as they bathed her in the brilliant white light that showed the entire audience she didn't know what on earth she was doing.

Somehow, she improvised a few steps; but her toe caught in something, the edge of the trap door on the stage, and she tripped and nearly fell flat on her face. Someone in the audience sniggered, and Kate's face flamed with embarrassment. Then, suddenly, she was furious. *It's all right for you!* she thought. *You're sitting down there all nice and cosy. Nobody's looking at you. I bet you wouldn't think it was so funny if you were up here instead of me!*

She pulled a face in the direction of the snigger and improvised more steps. There were more laughs from the audience, and a boy's voice saying clearly, 'Look, it's the Dance of the Sugar Plum Fatty!' The voice was instantly shushed, but it was too late. Even more people started to laugh. Kate gritted her teeth, and carried on; she could remember her dance now but it was no good, the

181

mood was ruined. So instead she stuck out her bottom, like a duck, and just made the thing up as she went along. *I may as well give them something to laugh at,* she thought furiously. *Rotten lot. I should never have let Uncle Nicholas talk me into doing this. I should have known I'd only end up looking stupid.*

Somehow, she got to the end of the dance, and as the last notes died away she bowed hastily (Miss Braithwaite had drummed it into her pupils never to leave a stage without bowing), and rushed from the stage, tears of disappointment and humiliation pricking her eyes and nearly blinding her.

She didn't hear the burst of applause that followed her exit. She didn't hear Mrs Voysey say, 'Well done, Kate!' as she brushed past her, and then, to Mr Penrose, 'I never knew that Burtons child had so much go about her! She really was amusing. The audience just loved her, once they realized she was being intentionally funny!'

Mr Penrose didn't reply. He knew Kate hadn't been intentionally funny. But he didn't tell that to Mrs Voysey; he thought it better that she thought what she thought.

Kate ran through the wings and into the room behind the stage. She wanted to hide herself away, to be alone and by herself and not have to explain to anyone what she had done and why she had done it. She was sure everyone would be furious with her for ruining the concert. The Pied Piper playlet was on next, and all the rats were milling around, squeaking like the animals they were supposed to represent. Peggy had lost her tail, and everyone else was tripping over all the other tails, trying to look for it. Nobody noticed Kate as she slipped through the small door in the corner of the room. The door led down some rickety stairs to the space under the stage. It was used for storing things – props and costumes – and was low-ceilinged, dark and dusty. It was also strictly out of bounds.

Kate crawled along to the end, not sure how low the ceiling was and not wishing to bump her head. She crouched there for a while, not moving, letting her eyes grow accustomed to the dim light which filtered in from the trap door above her head, and other cracks. She could still hear what was going on above her, and the response of the audience, but it was muted, muffled, rather like being under water. She made out the outline of a low wicker hamper; it was full of old dusty velvet curtains. She climbed in on top of them and curled up into a ball. She screwed her eyes shut and put her hands over her ears. She didn't want to see, she didn't want to hear, she didn't even want to think. She just wanted to vanish without trace.

15
After the Dance

It was Mr Penrose who came to find her. She heard him come down the stairs, despite the fingers stuffed in her ears, and he banged his head on the low ceiling and swore.

He bent over the hamper Kate was lying in, and put a hand on her shoulder.

'Kate,' he said. 'Kate. There you are.'

Kate gave a huge sigh. She unstopped her ears and opened her eyes. Mr Penrose had a torch, and its beam dazzled her; she squealed, and shaded her eyes with her hand.

'Sorry.' Mr Penrose snapped it off, and they were left in the darkness again. Kate felt the hamper sag as the teacher sat down beside her, and she held her breath, waiting for the scolding she was sure she was going to get. *What on earth did you think you were playing at, messing up the concert like that? Everyone's furious with you. And then running away afterwards – what a coward you are, Kate Burtons! Well, your aunt and uncle and cousins don't want you, and we're not surprised, because we don't want you either! We don't want cowards who can't even do a simple dance at a simple concert in* this *school!*

But the telling-off never came. Mr Penrose

didn't speak for a long time, and when he did, his voice was gentle.

'I've come to fetch you. Don't be frightened; you won't get into trouble, I promise.'

Kate didn't reply. She didn't believe him.

'Kate . . .'

'I can't. I feel sick inside.'

'I know.'

'Can't I just stay here?'

'You must go home. Everyone's worried.'

'I can't. I can't!'

'You must.'

'Can't you just say you couldn't find me, or that I was ill suddenly and had to go to hospital – or something?'

'You can't run away forever.'

And Kate knew he was right. Suddenly, she heard Aunt Rachel's voice, loud inside her head. *Your problems aren't with us, they're inside you. You can't run away from them.* She realized that she had been trying to run away from them right from the beginning. *The Granny Plan, and then rushing off to Dartmoor in a huff, and now this.* But running away was the only way she could think of to cope with things; to blank them out, pretend they didn't exist. She didn't know what she was going to do now.

On the way home in the car, they all looked at her with patient, pitying faces (all except Ned, who smirked), but nobody spoke to her. She was glad. She didn't want them to speak to her. She went to bed as soon as they were back, uncharacteristically leaving her clothes where they lay on the floor and

185

putting her nightie on inside out. A great weariness had enveloped her. She turned down Aunt Rachel's offer of cocoa, and fell asleep almost before her head touched the pillow.

She woke up later with a start, her mouth dry and her heart pounding. She didn't know what had woken her. Across the room, she could make out Charley, snoring blissfully under her duvet, and the digital clock beside Charley's bed, which said 11:58 in large red glowing numbers. *Nearly midnight. The Witching Hour. I must have been having a bad dream.* She took a few deep breaths until her heartbeat slowed to a more normal pace, and decided she wouldn't be able to get back to sleep until she had had a drink. *Perhaps I'll go and make that cocoa, after all.*

She swung her legs over the bed and padded downstairs, barefoot. Outside the kitchen door she stopped; she had thought everyone would be in bed at this hour, but light spilled from under the door and she could make out two murmuring voices – Aunt Rachel's and Uncle Nicholas's. She crept forward; she didn't intend to eavesdrop, but she had a sudden, certain knowledge they were talking about her.

At first, she couldn't make out what they were saying. Then, quite clearly, she heard Aunt Rachel say, 'Utterly useless, she really is.' Kate was frozen with horror. *So that's what they really think of me!* Then one of the dogs whined, and she couldn't hear what Uncle Nicholas replied.

But what Aunt Rachel said next was plain enough. 'It's hopeless, Nicky. I'm sorry, I know you thought you were helping, but I can't stand the chaos any more. She'll have to go.'

Kate's heart leapt to her throat. She couldn't move. Then the dog whined again, and scratched at the door.

'What's the matter, Max?' A chair scraped as Uncle Nicholas pushed it back, and his voice grew louder as he approached the door. 'What can you hear? What's out there, boy?'

Kate leapt back as if electrocuted, and fled up the stairs, terrified of being discovered.

Uncle Nicholas flung the door open and the dog shot out, sniffing around noisily and wagging his tail. 'Satisfied now? I think this place must be haunted; you're always scenting people who aren't there.'

He went back into the kitchen, followed reluctantly by the dog, who knew what he'd smelled was no ghost, and shut the door behind him. 'It's a real pity,' Uncle Nicholas went on, sitting down again at the table. 'I thought you'd find her a real help; you always seem so busy, and Brenda Bunson swears by her.'

'Whereas I just feel like swearing at her.' Aunt Rachel laughed ruefully, and patted her husband's hand. 'It was a lovely idea, darling, and very thoughtful of you. But it just isn't working out. Mrs Sadler's far too organized for the likes of me. And she disapproves totally of me. I feel I have to clean up before she gets here; I'm too ashamed to let her see the usual tip. She's like something out of a book; "Ay don't do curtains," she told me, "end Ay don't do pictures," whatever that's supposed to mean. And she presented me with a great long list of all the things she needs – special polishes and sprays and whatnot. And when I just made a casual remark about hoping they were ozone-friendly, she gave me such a dirty look. All Her Ladies get them for her, she told me, and none of the others have ever complained. And she keeps putting things away in the wrong places – do you know where I found Kate's dancing things this evening?' Uncle Nicholas shook his head. 'Under the stairs, of all places! What she was thinking of, I'll never know. Oh, and another thing –'

Uncle Nicholas raised his hands in surrender. 'Enough already! I get the picture. I'll tell her her services are no longer required. Just so long as that's what you really want.'

'It's what I really want.' Aunt Rachel smiled at him. 'We can't afford her, anyway. But it was sweet of you to arrange it, Nicky. Bless you.'

Her husband raised her hand to his lips and kissed it. 'I worry about you sometimes. You have so much on your plate; the house, and the kids, and the way you took Kate on without a murmur.'

Aunt Rachel pulled a face. 'That hasn't exactly been an unqualified success, though, has it? Poor child. You know, I feel really dreadful about what I said to her the other day, that she was stuck with us, and we with her. Perhaps I ought to have a chat with her – you know, woman to woman. Tell her it was just the heat of the moment, being worried about her. And Edward, of course. I had the most awful visions of them both drowned in a ditch, or something.'

'I did explain to her that you'd been dreadfully worried, and she seemed to understand. Trouble is, you never can tell with Kate; her face never gives anything away. Still, a bit of plain speaking probably did her good. And we've had no tantrums since, have we?'

Aunt Rachel sighed. 'I suppose not. But she did disappear for ages after the concert this evening. I don't entirely believe Mr Penrose's story about her helping the others to take their make-up off.'

'But she was all right when she did reappear, wasn't she?'

'I'm not so sure. She didn't say a word in the car. And she went straight off to bed when we got home.'

'I expect she was tired; she looked shattered. Anyway, if you want to have a word with her, I think you ought. But personally, I think you're worrying too much. She's doing OK, is Kate.' He chuckled suddenly. 'She was brilliant this evening, wasn't she? I really thought she'd botched the whole thing up and was going to run off the stage in tears, and then she turned the whole thing into a comic routine. I nearly died laughing!'

'She's certainly a trouper.' Aunt Rachel smiled. 'I wouldn't have had the guts to do what she did, that's for sure. I'd have wanted the ground to open up and swallow me. But I'm not convinced ballet's her thing, are you?'

Uncle Nicholas shook his head. 'Not really. But music; that's another matter.'

'Music?' Aunt Rachel was surprised. 'What makes you think that? She doesn't play, does she?'

'Not yet, no. But she's got a smashing singing voice; I kept hearing her singing that Debussy in the bathroom, and in the right key too, more often than not. And she picked it out on the piano that evening, do you remember? That was in the right key, as well.' Uncle Nicholas looked thoughtful. 'I wouldn't be surprised if she's got perfect pitch.'

'What will you do – ask her if she wants to learn an instrument?'

'I've got a better idea than that. It strikes me – it's always struck me – that our Kate hasn't got a very high opinion of herself. She needs to be good at something, something which is hers, to build up some self-respect.'

Aunt Rachel nodded slowly. 'I'm sure you're right. She doesn't actually like herself very much, does she? Only it gets all jumbled up inside her and comes out as her not liking other people. But she got very enthusiastic over doing that dance, didn't she? She was a changed person, for days on end. And then she had to spoil it by rushing off in a huff and getting herself and Edward lost.' She sighed. 'If only – if only we could get through to her that she's a worthwhile person, and that we all like her, and that we want to love her, if only she'd let herself be loved.'

'That's Mother,' Uncle Nicholas said ruefully. 'She never let herself be loved, either. And Patricia was probably the same. It's in the genes, Rach; and she's got twelve years of a totally different upbringing to cope with, too. Her previous life must have been so different. As I said, I've got an idea. I'll talk to her about it tomorrow. But now,' he said, pushing back his chair and standing up, 'it's late, and it's bedtime. It'll all have to wait until the morning.'

In the morning, Kate didn't want to get up. All she could think of was her aunt's words of the previous night. *She's utterly useless. She'll have to go.* She couldn't get them out of her mind. She felt exactly the same as she had that first morning at Appleford House, not wanting to face the day ahead. *No. Not the same – worse. Much worse. At least then I had some idea of what was going to happen. Not like now. What am I going to do? Where am I going to go?*

She turned over to face the wall and wouldn't answer Charley when she asked what the matter was.

'Kate?' It was Aunt Rachel. 'What's wrong? Don't you feel well?'

'No,' Kate mumbled, not turning over.

But Aunt Rachel made her sit up, and felt her forehead with a cool, solicitous hand. 'Well, you're not running a temperature, at any rate. I'll tell you what – come down and have some breakfast, and if you're still feeling poorly after that you can stay off school. Uncle Nicholas is in the kitchen; he's got the morning off too, he's got to go to the dentist. He wants a chat. Put your dressing gown on and come on down.'

Kate's insides heaved. *I know what he wants to chat to me about*, she thought wildly. *The Alternative Arrangement.*

'I feel sick,' she called out, quite truthfully, but it was too late. Aunt Rachel had already gone downstairs.

Somehow, she got herself out of bed and into her slippers and dressing gown. Then she did as she was bid and went downstairs. Everyone was sitting round the table, eating breakfast, and the cats were weaving about Aunt Rachel's ankles, crying pitifully for some kipper. They all ignored Kate, apart

191

from Uncle Nicholas, who smiled at her. He didn't look as if he was about to tell her she had to leave.

But his words turned her insides to ice. 'Ah, Kate,' he said. 'Come and sit down. I think it's time we had a little chat about what you're going to do with yourself.'

Kate sat down heavily on a chair. The tabby cat jumped instantly on to her lap and wound himself round, purring happily. She started to stroke the soft fur almost mechanically. *I have to tell him*, Kate thought, her stomach churning. *I have to tell him that I don't want to go anywhere else, that I want to stay here. I have to tell him that I'll try really, really hard to settle down here, and promise that I'll be good and not cause any more chaos. And I have to tell him that the reason I want to stay here is because I feel I could belong. Maybe not now – it's still too soon – but one day. I feel I could be part of the family. If only they would give me a bit more time. I know I've been a real pain, and acted as if I hate them all, but I don't really. I like them. I really do. I have to tell Uncle Nicholas that I like him, and I like Aunt Rachel, and I – I like everybody. I have to tell him all this, because it's true.*

Kate took a deep breath and opened her mouth to speak. Only what came out wasn't words, but a sort of strangled squeak. Then she burst into tears.

16

My Heart Ever Faithful

Once she started to cry she thought she would never stop. It was like a dam bursting. Water seemed to be coming from everywhere; from her eyes, her nose, her mouth. She put her hands over her face to try and stop the flood of tears, but they spurted through her fingers. Her head felt as if it would burst. She couldn't catch her breath, and her hands were sliding over the tears on her face.

She raised her head to look at Aunt Rachel, and managed to gasp, 'I don't want to go away! I don't want to go away!'

'But Kate,' she heard her aunt reply, in a gentle voice, 'you don't have to. You don't have to go anywhere. You can stay right here with me.'

She felt herself being sat down on a chair, and strong warm arms going round her, and she buried her face against a shoulder and howled and sobbed and wept until she thought her heart would truly break. It seemed to go on for ever.

Someone began to rock her gently, and to stroke her hair with tender, rhythmic strokes, the way she herself had been stroking the cat. It was very soothing. Gradually, the storm of weeping began to subside, until with a final hiccup the flow of tears stopped, as though turned off like a tap. Kate felt exhausted, as if every last drop of her energy had flowed out of her with her tears. Her face felt bloated, its tissues swollen with all that water pouring down it.

When at last she took her hands from her face she saw that all the cousins had melted from the room, and she was alone with Uncle Nicholas and Aunt Rachel. Her aunt was kneeling on the floor in front of her. She put a hand under Kate's chin and tilted it, and looked deep into her eyes. Her own eyes were serious and compassionate.

'Kate,' she said sombrely, 'I promise that you never again have to go anywhere you don't want to go. Do you trust me?' Kate nodded, and her aunt leant forward and touched Kate's forehead with her lips. 'Good. Now do you want to tell us where you thought we were sending you?'

It took a long time for Kate to answer. 'Away,' she said at last. 'Just away. I don't know where, exactly. An orphanage, I suppose.'

'But why?' Uncle Nicholas sounded bemused. 'Why would we do that?'

Kate didn't know where to begin. It all seemed so obvious to her, she couldn't believe they really didn't know. 'Well,' she said. 'There was the Granny Plan, and all those lies I told. And then taking Edward on Dartmoor and Aunt Rachel being so cross. And I haven't been very nice, have I? And then the concert yesterday, and mucking it all up. And then I heard you last night' – she gulped, and went on – 'saying I had to go.'

Her aunt and uncle looked at each other, horrified.

194

'What?' said Uncle Nicholas. He sounded shocked. 'When did we say that?'

'Last night,' Kate repeated. 'I came down for a drink and heard you talking. You said I was useless,' she added, and the thought nearly started her crying again.

Light dawned on her aunt's face. 'We weren't talking about you at all!' she exclaimed. 'I was sounding off about Mrs Sadler – you know, the new cleaning lady who hid your dancing things. I was telling Nicky I couldn't stand her any more. It's her who has to go, not you!' She saw the relief on Kate's face. 'Oh, sweetheart! You didn't really think we meant you, did you?' Kate nodded, mutely, and her aunt pressed her against her shoulder and murmured things into her hair. The strange thing was, Kate didn't feel at all uncomfortable. It was quite nice, being cuddled and rocked like a baby. It was comforting.

'Anyway,' said Uncle Nicholas, 'you didn't muck the concert up last night. Far from it.'

'But I forgot my dance!' Kate protested, struggling to sit up. 'Everybody was laughing at me!'

Aunt Rachel shook her head. 'You carried on,' she said softly. 'That takes courage. You carried on.'

Kate looked at them both suspiciously. 'But everyone laughed,' she repeated stubbornly. 'It was awful. I didn't know what to do.'

'They laughed because you were funny – really funny! People were laughing with you, not at you. Can't you see that?'

Uncle Nicholas nodded. 'It's true,' he said. 'You

were good, Kate. Everyone thought so. Honestly.'

Kate carried on staring at them, not daring to believe that what they said was true. Then her face softened, and a slight smile curved her mouth.

'Was I?' she said, softly. 'Was I really?' She suddenly thought of something, and the thought made her get down from the chair in a hurry and stand facing them both.

'What did you mean,' she asked Uncle Nicholas accusingly, 'about having a chat about what I was going to do?'

'Not what you obviously thought I meant,' he said reassuringly. 'I had no idea you thought we were going to send you away, or I would have put it differently. We didn't mean to frighten you, Kate; you're going to live here with us, there's no question of anything else.'

'Not an orphanage?' Kate's voice was very small.

Aunt Rachel sounded fierce. 'Under no circumstances! You're family, Kate. And we want you here. You've had a tough time. I understand.'

'You can't,' Kate said angrily. She didn't understand, herself; how could Aunt Rachel? 'You can't understand. I loved my. . . . I loved them. And they loved me too. It was just them, and me. And now it's just me, and I'm never going to see them again, not ever. No matter how much I want to, I shall never see them again. But I shall always love them.'

'Of course you will,' Aunt Rachel said softly.

Kate went on. 'And just because I like it here and like all you lot and everything, it doesn't mean I'm going to forget about them, because I'm not. Never ever ever!'

Aunt Rachel took her hand. 'I really do understand,' she said again. 'My own mother died when I was fourteen. My father had divorced her when I was six, and she'd brought me up by herself since then. I was fostered out until I went to university, and then I fended for myself. I got used to my new life, without my mother, but I never stopped missing her. I still miss her, even now. But I don't feel guilty any more about enjoying life, because I know that's what my mum would have wanted. She wouldn't have wanted me to mope around feeling miserable and putting my own life on the back burner because she was no longer around to share it with me. So you see, I do know how you feel.'

Kate had had no idea that Aunt Rachel had gone through an experience so similar to her own. It came as quite a shock.

'But knowing you understand doesn't help,' she said slowly. 'I know it should, but it doesn't. I don't think anything will help. I don't think I shall ever feel like me again.'

'Yes, you will,' her aunt told her. 'Just give yourself time. Time is a tremendous help. And don't be so hard on yourself. You've had a dreadful shock about your parents, you've been uprooted from everything you know and sent to live in this madhouse' – a small smile flickered over Kate's face at this – 'and your whole life has changed out of all recognition. Of course it's going to take time for you to adjust. If you would only accept that, you'd find things much easier. And everyone wants to help, you know, if you would just let them.'

'Talking will help,' said Uncle Nicholas gently.

'Bottling things up, all these sad and angry feelings, will just make you feel worse. And crying will help too, you know, if you feel like it.'

'I never cry,' Kate said fiercely. 'Crying's for little kids. It's silly. I only cried just now because –'

'It's not silly at all,' her uncle interrupted her. 'It's very sensible. What's silly is trying to keep a stiff upper lip when you're upset. We all cry when we're upset.'

'Even you?' It was hard to believe.

'Especially me. You just ask your aunt. I'm a proper old cry-baby.'

Kate stared at him. She couldn't imagine him crying. She had never seen her father look particularly unhappy, let alone cry.

He smiled encouragingly at her. Kate looked at her aunt and uncle for a long moment, trying to work out how she felt. All at once, her body sagged with tiredness. *I'm fed up trying to work out my feelings all the time. Why can't I just feel them, like normal people do, without trying to understand them?* She suddenly felt tremendous relief, as if she had discovered the answer to a problem which had been bothering her for a long time. Then she realized that she felt better. Only a little bit, but definitely better. It was as though a knot inside her had been loosened slightly, ready to be properly untied.

'I think you should sing,' Uncle Nicholas said suddenly, out of the blue.

Kate was puzzled. 'Pardon?'

'What I was talking about – what you should do with yourself. I think you're very musical, Kate, only you've never had the chance to discover it. I'd like to give you singing lessons, if you'll let me. Will you think about it?'

She didn't have to think about it for very long. What she wanted to do, her automatic response, was to say 'Oh, yes please!' as soon as Uncle Nicholas offered. She had known nothing at all about music before she came to Appleford House, had scarcely ever heard any 'serious music', as her mother had called it, but ever since hearing Gus play the Liszt sonata at his school concert it seemed to her that music possessed certain mystical powers. It had certainly had a magical effect on her that night, and by all accounts on the rest of the audience too. She would have given anything to be able to play like that, to have that kind of power over people, to have them clap and cheer and say, 'isn't she wonderful?'

But she knew that you had to start piano lessons when you were very young to be as good as Gus, and here she was, turned twelve, and no knowledge of music whatsoever. And now Uncle Nicholas was offering to teach her how to sing properly!

She may have wanted to say yes instantly, but she didn't. She didn't want them to think that, just because they had seen her crying, with her defences down, she was in future going to agree with everything they said and fall in with all their plans. She didn't want them to feel sorry for her, and to offer to help out of pity. And she didn't want them to think that they were now all going to live happily ever after with each other. She wasn't sure that they were, necessarily. She felt better, it was true, but not *that* much better. *It happens like that in books*, she thought wistfully. *There's a big scene and everyone cries, and then everything turns out all right. You can always turn to the end of a book, when you're reading it, to see that things work out, so if they don't you don't have to read it and get upset. I wish I could look into the future and see how things are going to work out.*

After two days of thinking these thoughts, she went to Uncle Nicholas.

'I would like singing lessons, please. If you still want to teach me,' she added.

So she started having lessons. Most evenings, after school, she and Uncle Nicholas would go to the music room and he would teach her. He drove her hard, but Kate enjoyed it. She soaked up everything he told her, like a sponge, and came back for more; she enjoyed the feeling it gave her, the sense of achievement. He taught her how to sing smoothly from low notes to high ones, so that her voice didn't swoop and 'change gear' in the middle. He taught her how to pronounce the words clearly. 'You must emphasize your consonants,' he told her, bafflingly. 'People want to hear what you're singing about, not a meaningless blur.' He left her singing alone by the piano and prowled around the back of the room, shouting out every time he couldn't understand a word.

He taught her how to tackle high notes: 'Don't stretch and strain up to them – pretend you're reaching down on to them from above' – and how to 'centre' her voice, pretending it was coming out from the top of her head, so that she produced a pure, clear tone. He gave her scales to sing – endless ladders of notes rising up and down – and breathing exercises to fill and empty her lungs in the correct way. He taught her the basic theory of music, crotchets and quavers and minims, Every Green Bus Drives Fast and FACE, clefs and staves and bar lines, key signatures and time signatures, and then incomprehensible things with impossible names that Uncle Nicholas would rattle off like an Italian menu – *acciaccatura*, *cantabile*, *anacrucis*, *rallentando*.

But most of all, he taught her to listen.

'The trouble with most people,' he told her, 'is that they don't use their ears properly. You must be listening constantly – to check whether you're in tune, whether you're in time, whether you blend properly, particularly if you're singing or playing with other people. What do you think is the most important part of your body in music?'

After all the talk about listening, there could only be one answer.

'Your ears,' said Kate.

Uncle Nicholas beamed. 'Your ears. Exactly!'

So, as well as the singing, they would sit in the music room and Uncle Nicholas would put on records: organ music by Bach, Mozart operas, Beethoven symphonies, and choral music that was four hundred years old – 'Tudor church music', Kate learned to call it. She sat and listened, and thought she had never heard anything so beautiful in her life.

Charley thought Kate was mad.

'You must be potty,' she told her, 'letting Dad teach you. Mum had driving lessons from him once – or rather, driving lesson. She said he shouted at her so much when she made mistakes she couldn't stand it any more, and she paid for proper lessons.'

'He doesn't shout at me,' Kate said smugly. He did, actually, but strangely, it didn't put her off. *At least he's being honest*, she thought. *It makes a change from all the pussyfooting around me that people have been doing.* And he wasn't slow to praise her when she did things to his satisfaction.

'You must be getting on OK,' Ned told her gloomily one evening. 'He was yelling at us lot this morning for singing something wrong – said his niece would show the lot of us up, and she's only been learning a couple of weeks.'

Kate bristled. She was still wary of Ned. 'Sorry,' she said. 'But it's not my fault.'

'Never said it was,' Ned said irritably. 'Don't get out of your pram!'

One weekend when Gus came home, he was standing outside the music room at lunchtime on Saturday when Uncle Nicholas and Kate came out.

'Hello,' he greeted them. 'Has Dad got you practising on Saturdays too? What a slave-driver. Mum sent me to fetch you for lunch.'

'Not a bit of it,' his father said cheerfully. 'She loves it, don't you, my deario? Come on up then, Kate. If Rachel sent Gus to fetch us, she'll be dishing up by now.'

He went along the corridor and Kate made to follow him, but Gus stopped her.

'Don't let Dad bully you,' he told her, in a low voice. 'He does tend to overdo it a bit where music's concerned – he's like an out-of-control Exocet. If you don't want to do it, just say so.'

'Oh, no,' Kate assured him. 'It's fine. I like it, honestly.'

'That's OK, then. What were you singing – Bach, was it?'

Kate nodded. ' "My Heart Ever Faithful." '

'Thought so.' Gus regarded his cousin thoughtfully. 'You know, it sounded really good. Really – accomplished. I reckon you've got something.'

Kate looked at Gus, surprised. Then she smiled, a proper smile that reached her eyes. If Gus thought she sounded good then she must do. He knew about music.

17
Honorary Fred

When Kate had been having lessons from Uncle Nicholas for about three weeks, he had a proposition for her.

'How would you like to sing in the school concert?' he asked her, casually.

At first, she thought he was joking. 'Ha ha,' she said. 'Anyway, we've had the concert – I did that stupid dance, remember?' *Don't say he's forgotten about it already. I shall never forget it, not as long as I live.*

But he wasn't joking. 'Not St Mary's concert. *Our* concert.'

She stared at him. 'Your concert? You mean here, at Appleford House?'

'Where else?' He was smiling at her.

'But I can't – I don't go to school here! Anyway, I'm not good enough.'

Kate thought that was the end of the matter, but it wasn't.

'Oh, you're good enough,' Uncle Nicholas assured her. 'Make no mistake about that.'

He explained that every year at the end-of-term concert, there was a surprise item on the programme. 'Someone connected with the school does their party-piece – it's usually a parent or a new member of staff. We call it the "Surprise Guest Artiste" number.'

'Someone gets up and sings a song?'

'Not always – it varies from year to year. Last year one of the parents did some conjuring. The year before we had morris dancing. We've had piano solos, violin solos, flute solos, every instrumental solo you can think of; we've had poetry and one-act plays, folk music. One year we even had a jazz band. Jolly good they were, too.'

'I'm not sure.' Kate frowned. 'Do I have to?'

'Of course not.' Uncle Nicholas doodled on the piano. 'I thought it would give you something to work towards – a goal, if you like. But you don't have to if you don't want to. Think about it.'

Kate thought. 'When is it?'

'Didn't I tell you? Friday – next week.'

Kate was torn. On the one hand, she quite liked the idea of performing the Bach piece they had been working on, properly performing it, instead of just beavering away at it and then putting it away and starting on something new. As Uncle Nicholas had said, it would give her a goal to work towards. He was very keen on goals, and didn't much enjoy working on something for its own sake. 'Music in a vacuum', he called it.

On the other hand, Kate was very nervous at the idea of doing something in public again after the last time. She still thought her dance had been a disaster. *Even if they were laughing with me, as Aunt Rachel said, they were still laughing. And I still forgot how it went; after all that practising! I couldn't bear it if that happened again. I would just die, I know I would.*

She talked to Tamzin about it at school. They were in the cloakroom, getting changed for PE.

'My uncle wants me to sing in his school concert,' she told her, 'and I don't know whether to or not.'

Tamzin looked at her with interest. 'I didn't know you could sing!' she exclaimed. 'Sing something for us – go on!'

Kate went red with embarrassment. 'No – no, I can't, really, I've only been doing it for a few weeks. . . .' She felt stupid.

But Tamzin didn't seem to notice. 'Well, you must be OK if your uncle's asked you, mustn't you? He's a music teacher, isn't he? He must reckon you're all right.'

'He does,' said Charley, who had been listening. 'He reckons she's brilliant. He's always going on about her; we're all getting sick of the sound of her name!' But it wasn't said spitefully, and she smiled at Kate, to show she didn't mean it.

'I think you should do it,' Tamzin said definitely.

'But what if I forget how it goes? I'll feel really daft – like when I did that stupid dance,' she added.

'What dance?' Tamzin looked puzzled. 'You mean, the one at our concert? But you didn't forget that. Everyone clapped like mad when you finished.'

'I still forgot it,' Kate said gloomily. 'It was supposed to be a serious dance, about the moon, but when the music started I forgot what I was supposed to be doing, and just made it up as I went along.'

'You never!' Peggy was wide-eyed. 'My dad reckoned it was the best thing in that concert – he laughed for a week. "That Kate must be a proper comedy hen", he kept saying.'

'Comedienne,' Kate corrected her. 'Did he really think it was good?'

'It was good,' Tamzin assured her. 'And I think you should sing in your uncle's concert if he's asked you to. Look, are you going to be my partner for PE this week? Mrs Voysey said we're doing the vaulting horse again, and you're much better than me.'

Kate looked a bit doubtful. 'If Charley doesn't mind; you know we're usually partners.'

'Why should I mind?' Charley shook her head emphatically and did up her plimsolls. 'You're hopeless; I don't know why Tamzin said you're better than her.'

Peggy looked shocked. 'Charley! Don't be rotten! She is good on the horse – you are, Kate, don't take any notice of her.'

But Charley just laughed. 'She knows I'm only joking, don't you, Kate? She doesn't mind.'

Kate was surprised to find she really didn't mind. 'It's all right,' she told Peggy. 'I knew she didn't mean it. We're cousins. We don't have to be nice to each other all the time.'

'We break up next week,' Charley said suddenly. 'No more pukey school for weeks and weeks, isn't it brill! Have Mum and Dad told you we're going camping in France this year?'

'France!' Tamzin looked envious. 'You lucky things, I've never been abroad; well, I've been to the Isle of Wight, but that docsn't really count.'

207

'I'll tell you all about it next term,' Kate assured her.

'You'll have to come to tea,' said Tamzin. 'Mum keeps on at me to invite you, but I keep forgetting. Would you like to?'

'I'd love to,' said Kate. 'I'll look forward to it.'

That evening, Kate told Uncle Nicholas she would sing in the concert.

'Just so long as you're sure I'll be OK,' she said nervously.

'I'm sure.'

'Promise?'

'Cross my heart and hope to die.'

'What'll happen if I forget the words?'

'There's no need to do it from memory unless you want to. You can have the music if you like.'

'But what'll happen if –'

'Kate.' Uncle Nicholas put a kindly hand on her shoulder. 'You are a worrier. You'll be perfectly all right, I promise you. And I'll be there too, remember; I'll be accompanying you. But if it worries you that much, perhaps you'd rather not do it, after all.'

'Oh, no,' said Kate hastily. 'I've said I will, so I will.'

But despite Uncle Nicholas's reassurances, Kate still worried. Three days before the concert, she awoke with a sore throat.

'It's flu!' she cried to Aunt Rachel. 'I've got flu! Oh, what am I going to do? I'll never be able to sing in the concert now!'

'Calm down,' her aunt told her. 'I doubt very

much that it's flu. Do you feel hot, or have you got a headache or any other aches and pains?'

Kate shook her head. 'But my ears feel all bunged up. They keep popping.'

'I had that,' Harry said with pride. 'The doctor said it was my Euston Station tubes. I had to breathe in stinky stuff in hot water to un-bung them, didn't I, Mummy? I had to have a towel over my head.'

'You did,' said Aunt Rachel. 'In fact, I think that's a very good idea. Come on, Kate.' And she made Kate do the same thing. It did help, Kate had to admit. Aunt Rachel brought her breakfast in bed; she dosed her up and told her to stay in bed, and by lunchtime her throat felt a bit better, too.

'It's probably just a bit of a cold,' Aunt Rachel told her. 'I'm sure you'll be feeling perfectly OK by Friday. Anyway, don't you go worrying yourself about it; there'll always be another time!'

But Kate didn't want another time. She wanted to sing in that particular concert, on Friday. She'd got herself all mentally prepared for it.

In the afternoon, Aunt Rachel made up a bed on the sofa for her.

'Here you are,' she said. 'You don't want to stay in that bedroom all by yourself all day. I've got a mound of ironing to do; you can keep me company.'

It was quite cosy, reclining on the sofa, swathed in duvet, while the room filled with the fresh smell of ironing. It was quiet, too, with the older cousins at school and Edward having a nap, but Kate couldn't settle.

'It's just typical,' she brooded out loud. 'Something always happens to spoil things. I suppose it's my fault for looking forward to it.'

'Were you looking forward to it?' Aunt Rachel folded a blouse. 'I'm glad. Nicky tells me you're coming on beautifully. I can't wait to hear you.'

'I *was* looking forward to it. I don't suppose I'll be able to do it now; I always seem to ruin everything.'

Aunt Rachel frowned. 'How d'you mean?'

'Oh, I don't know; things never go the way I want them to. My old teacher used to say that you should never wish for things too much, or they'll never happen.'

'That's one way of looking at things. But then there are people who say that wanting a thing badly enough can *make* it happen.'

Kate flushed, and bit her lip. Aunt Rachel looked at her curiously.

'What's wrong?' she asked her.

'Nothing.' Kate turned her face away.

'It doesn't look like nothing,' her aunt said gently. 'Come on, Kate – tell me what's wrong.'

'It's just. . . .' Kate sighed heavily, and wouldn't look Aunt Rachel in the eye. 'Can you make people die, d'you think?'

Aunt Rachel was startled. 'How d'you mean?'

'Can you wish them dead? I mean, can you wish for it to happen and then it does?'

There was a long silence. Then Aunt Rachel said, 'Is this about your parents?'

Kate looked up at last, and their eyes met. She nodded.

Aunt Rachel put down the iron and sat on the edge of the sofa. 'Kate,' she said. 'You weren't to blame for your parents' death. They died in a car accident. You know that.'

'Before they went,' Kate said slowly, 'I was upset. It was Christmas and they'd said we could go to a pantomime, and then they had to go on the business trip. I wished and wished that something would happen to stop them going, but nothing did. Then when they were away I wished and wished that something would happen to make them come back early.' She stopped, upset.

'And there were times,' she went on, 'when I was cross about something, that I wished they were dead. I know it's awful, but I did. And now they are. It must have been my fault.'

'Listen to me. We all feel that at times about people, particularly people we love. Love and hate are strong emotions, and if certain people have the power to make us love them, then they can make us hate them at times too. There's nothing wrong with that. But wishing someone dead can't make it happen.'

'Unless you're a witch.' Kate's eyes were large and frightened.

'Sweetheart, you're not a witch!'

'But how do you know I'm not?' Kate wailed.

Aunt Rachel put her arms around her. 'Because I do,' she said fiercely into Kate's hair. 'Don't feel guilty because you're alive and they're not. It's not your fault.' She said it over and over again, as if repeating it would make it true.

As Aunt Rachel had predicted, by Friday Kate's sore throat had gone. She went back to school that day.

'Are you better?' Tamzin asked her. 'Are you going to be able to sing in that concert?'

'Oh, yes,' Kate said definitely.

She was surprised at how calm she felt about it. Not nervous at all, not like before the St Mary's concert. Well, perhaps a bit. But Uncle Nicholas had told her that it was a good thing to feel a few butterflies beforehand.

'It shows everything's in working order,' he had said. 'Gets the adrenalin going.'

During supper that evening, Gus walked in. His appearance flustered Kate.

'What are you doing here?' she demanded. 'You come home on Saturdays!'

Gus grinned. 'Come to hear your famous Bach, haven't I?'

Aunt Rachel glanced anxiously at Kate. 'Don't tease her,' she scolded Gus. 'You'll make her nervous.'

'It's all right,' Kate assured everybody. 'I'm not nervous.' She was secretly quite pleased Gus was going to be there. He sat down at the table and pinched Ned's roll.

'Oi!' said Ned. 'Give that back!'

Gus stuffed it into his mouth. 'Not likely – I'm starving. Mum, do I have to come to poxy France with you lot next month? Damaris's parents are taking her to the States; she says I can go too, if I want.'

Kate and Charley exchanged looks.

'Who's Damaris?' Kate whispered.

'Who's Damaris?' Charley demanded loudly. 'And what's happened to *Petula*?' She put on a funny voice.

'Oh, she's a snooty cow,' said Gus offhandedly.

'You mean she's going out with someone else!' Ned crowed.

Gus flushed. 'That's got nothing to do with it. Anyway, Damaris is cool. She really understands me.'

'Oh, good grief!' Charley leant over the edge of the table and made loud retching noises. 'Pass the sick bag. Why do all the girls in your school have such gross names?'

Gus threw the remains of Ned's roll at her, and Edward chuckled with glee. He liked throwing things around at mealtimes, too.

'You're very quiet,' Aunt Rachel remarked to Harry. 'Don't tell me you've got a sore throat now.'

Harry shook his head. 'No,' he said glumly. 'Miss Maltby's getting married next Saturday. It's the last time I'll ever see her.'

'Why – won't Mr Christmas let her work?' Charley demanded. 'What a male chauvinist pig!'

'He's not a male show fist pig,' Harry protested. If his beloved Miss Maltby was to marry him, Mr Christmas must be all right, he'd decided. 'They're going to live in Carlisle. Where is Carlisle, Mummy?'

'The End of the Universe,' Ned pronounced, in doom-laden tones. Harry looked even more miserable.

'Cheer up,' whispered Kate, putting a hand over his. 'You wouldn't have been in her class next year, anyway.'

Harry looked momentarily brighter, then slumped in his chair again. 'I'd still have seen her around school, though.'

Aunt Rachel sighed loudly, and they all looked at her. 'That's life, children,' she said wistfully. 'Everything changes. Nothing stays the same for long. Come on, Edward, it's time for your bath.'

After the concert, Kate could only marvel at how easy it had been. When Mr Bunson announced that she was to be the Surprise Guest Artiste, everyone started to clap. Kate stood up and began the long walk to the stage from her place in the audience. As she stood on the stage there was one dreadful moment of clammy, crawling panic while she remembered what had happened at the St Mary's concert. Then Uncle Nicholas smiled at her across the piano. 'Ready?' he whispered – and began to play the introduction, and she started to sing.

'My heart ever-faithful,' she sang. 'Sing praises, be joyful!' She realized there was no danger of her forgetting the words. They were ingrained in her memory for ever. She relaxed, and began to enjoy herself.

When the song was over, the audience clapped and cheered for more.

'What shall I do?' Kate whispered frantically to her uncle. 'I don't know any more!'

Uncle Nicholas held up his hand for silence. 'I'm afraid that's all you're getting,' he told the audience. 'Kate's had a bad throat, and I don't want her to strain it. Sorry!'

The audience clapped even more at this, obviously thinking that Kate had dragged herself from her sick-bed to perform for them, and she felt quite breathless when she finally left the stage and rejoined Aunt Rachel and the cousins. She glowed with pride at all the congratulations that were mouthed at her on her way back to her seat.

In the dining hall, when the concert was over, Uncle Nicholas brought her a big glass of orange.

'Here you are,' he said. 'It should be champagne, by rights, but I'm afraid this is all I could find.'

'Didn't she do well?' Aunt Rachel beamed. 'Aren't you proud of her?'

'You should be, Dad,' Gus put in. 'She was brill. Stood up there like a pro. Well done, Kate!'

'I think you were super-brill,' Charley told her breathlessly. 'I don't know how you could sing in front of all those people. I couldn't.'

'You can't sing in the bath,' Ned told her bluntly.

Harry was hopping about from foot to foot. 'I think she was super-duper-brill!' he squeaked. 'Miss Maltby says you should always –' There was the customary groan.

People kept coming up to Kate and congratulating her, shaking her hand and smiling, and saying things to Uncle Nicholas about chips off old blocks. Her smile muscles began to ache.

'How does it feel to be famous?' Aunt Rachel asked her, with a smile.

Mr Bunson came over. 'Ah, Kathleen – the guest chanteuse,' he said, smiling and blinking at her behind his glasses. 'Another musical one, Nicholas. I can see you'll be grooming her for stardom. Well done, Kathleen.'

Kate opened her mouth to correct him. 'Kate,' she was about to say. But Ned got there first.

'Fred,' he said quietly, so quietly that at first Kate thought she'd misheard him.

So did Mr Bunson. 'I beg your pardon?' he said, smiling in a baffled way.

Ned cleared his throat. 'Fred, Sir,' he said politely to his headmaster. 'We call her Fred. It's a sort of nickname.'

'Ah, yes. Indeed,' Mr Bunson said vaguely. 'Well done, anyway, er – um – well done!' And he went off to talk to the chairman of the governors.

Everyone was staring at Ned. 'What on earth are you on about?' Gus demanded.

But Kate knew. 'It's the alphabet,' she said. 'Your names – you know, Augustus, Benedict . . .'

'Etc., etc., etc.,' Ned said. He turned to his father. 'You've always said that if there was another one of us, it'd have to be called Fred. And now there is. Well, an honorary Fred, at any rate.' He looked at Kate and smiled, and she suddenly realized he'd never smiled at her before. It was a nice smile. 'You did OK, ratbag,' he told her, and punched her on the arm. 'You did OK.'

And Kate knew that, of all the complimentary things that people had said to her that evening, what Ned had just said meant the most to her.

It's going to be all right, she told herself. *Nothing stays the same for ever. It's going to be all right.*

Other great reads from *Red Fox*

Discover the great animal stories of Colin Dann

JUST NUFFIN

The Summer holidays loomed ahead with nothing to look forward to except one dreary week in a caravan with only Mum and Dad for company. Roger was sure he'd be bored.

But then Dad finds Nuffin: an abandoned puppy who's more a bundle of skin and bones than a dog. Roger's holiday is transformed and he and Nuffin are inseparable. But Dad is adamant that Nuffin must find a new home. Is there *any* way Roger can persuade him to change his mind?

ISBN 0 09 966900 5   £2.99

KING OF THE VAGABONDS

'You're very young,' Sammy's mother said, 'so heed my advice. Don't go into Quartermile Field.'

His mother and sister are happily domesticated but Sammy, the tabby cat, feels different. They are content with their lot, never wondering what lies beyond their immediate surroundings. But Sammy is burningly curious and his life seems full of mysteries. Who is his father? Where has he gone? And what is the mystery of Quartermile Field?

ISBN 0 09 957190 0   £2.99

Other great reads **from Red Fox**

Haunting fiction for older readers from Red Fox

THE XANADU MANUSCRIPT
John Rowe Townsend

There is nothing unusual about visitors in Cambridge.

So what is it about three tall strangers which fills John with a mixture of curiosity and unease? Not only are they strikingly handsome but, for apparently educated people, they are oddly surprised and excited by normal, everyday events. And, as John pursues them, their mystery only seems to deepen.

Set against a background of an old university town, this powerfully compelling story is both utterly fantastic and oddly convincing.

'An author from whom much is expected and received.' *Economist*

ISBN 0 09 975180 1 £2.99

ONLOOKER Roger Davenport

Peter has always enjoyed being in Culver Wood, and dismissed the tales of hauntings, witchcraft and superstitions associated with it. But when he starts having extraordinary visions that are somehow connected with the wood, and which become more real to him than his everyday life, he realizes that something is taking control of his mind in an inexplicable and frightening way.

Through his uneasy relationship with Isobel and her father, a Professor of Archaeology interested in excavating Culver Wood, Peter is led to the discovery of the wood's secret and his own terrifying part in it.

ISBN 0 09 975070 8 £2.99